"No one has ever called me beautiful before."

"There's no doubt that you are tonight."

Slowly, she raised her eyes to meet his. Was it admiration she saw in their cold gray depths or mockery? She couldn't be sure, but she was certain he was going to kiss her, and every nerve in her body quivered in anticipation. His hands grasped her around the waist, and she moaned. When his lips met hers, she was ready, and her response was immediate. He couldn't fail to be aware of it. . . .

By Rachelle Edwards
Published by Fawcett Crest:

FORTUNE'S CHILD
THE MARRIAGE BARGAIN
THE SCOUNDREL'S DAUGHTER
DANGEROUS DANDY
AN UNEQUAL MATCH
REGENCY MASQUERADE
THE RANSOME INHERITANCE
LADY OF QUALITY
RUNAWAY BRIDE
SWEET HOYDEN
LUCIFER'S LADY
THE HIGHWAYMAN AND THE LADY
THE RAKE'S REVENGE
MARYLEBONE PARK
LOVE FINDS A WAY
MARRIAGE À LA MODE

MARRIAGE À LA MODE

Rachelle Edwards

FAWCETT CREST • NEW YORK

A Fawcett Crest Book
Published by The Ballantine Publishing Group
Copyright © 1998 by Rachelle Edwards

http://www.randomhouse.com

Library of Congress Catalog Card Number: 97-95284

ISBN 0-449-00341-8

Manufactured in the United States of America

First Edition: July 1998

10 9 8 7 6 5 4 3 2 1

MARRIAGE À LA MODE

Chapter One

"*It*'s no use, Molly. I just can't find a gown remotely suitable to wear for your mother's ball!"

Arabella Trentham's head was buried in the depths of her clothespress. When she emerged, specks of cotton and muslin peppered her fair curls, which were pinned up on top of her head in an untidy pile.

Molly Polstead, Arabella's young cousin, looked up from the book she was reading to observe in a bored tone, "If you can't find a *blue* gown, Bella, you'll be obliged to wear the white lutestring, even though the invitation stipulated it was going to be a Blue Ball."

"I know, although I didn't exactly receive an invitation," Arabella answered in despair, gazing at the outmoded garment draped across a chair.

"Mama only thought up the idea because blue becomes her so well, and she wants an opportunity to show off the Polstead sapphires."

"Whatever her reason for holding this diversion, Molly, it's certain I shall be the only female present who is wearing white."

"White is exceedingly modish."

"Not when blue is called for, and in any event white makes me look sallow, not that anyone will notice me. No one ever does," Arabella added in a wistful tone before she peered myopically across the room to where

1

her young cousin was sprawled across the bed, her nose in a book. All at once Arabella became animated. "Molly! Put it down this instant. You shouldn't be reading that book!"

She dashed across the room and snatched it from the girl's grasp, closing it with a snap, and slapping it down on the bedside table from which it had been purloined. "Such literature is not in the least suitable for someone of your tender years."

Molly swung her thin legs over the side of the bed. "How hateful you are, Bella. I'd just reached the part where Ramona was imprisoned in the castle by Count Lazlo, and Benedict had no notion where she might be."

"I'm quite sure he will find her in time," Arabella assured the child.

"In time for what?" the girl asked innocently, her plain little face frowning up into Arabella's.

"Never you mind! If your mama discovers you have been reading such nonsense, she'll fly up into the boughs and give me a severe wigging."

"You read those books all the time!"

"I'm an adult."

"Only just, Bella."

"As a poor relation, romantic novels are the closest I shall ever get to a grand passion, Molly, and you should not begrudge me the diversion."

The child looked aghast. "How dreadful for you. I do hope I won't be obliged to share your fate."

Arabella laughed. "No, dearest, I'm persuaded you won't. Recall I have neither looks nor fortune to recommend me."

"Whereas I, at least, will have fortune, which is just as well, for I shall never be a beauty."

"I am resigned to my fate," Arabella answered heroically.

"It must be odious to be like Ramona and compelled to

2

endure such fearsome adventures before finding true love."

Arabella flopped down onto the counterpane at her cousin's side. "I confess, I shouldn't mind in the least, as long as I knew I would be rescued by my one true love in the final chapter."

"Real life isn't like that," the girl replied with a maturity beyond her years.

"No, indeed it is not." Arabella sighed. "And I daresay it is just as well."

Molly's face puckered into an impish grin. "When I was reading *Prisoner of Desire*, I couldn't stop myself imagining Lord Carisbrooke as Benedict."

Arabella cast her a sharp look. "Lord Carisbrooke?"

"Well, he must be the most handsome man alive."

Arabella turned away when her cheeks started to feel warm. "I cannot say I have noticed."

"You must have done. Every debutante casts out lures in his direction."

"I am not a debutante, so you'll have to excuse my ignorance of Lord Carisbrooke."

"It would make no odds if you were a debutante; he's madly in love with Mama."

Arabella turned to her sharply once again. "Molly! You mustn't say such a thing! Your papa would be furious if he heard you."

"It's true, though, and Papa must know it too. Lord Carisbrooke is too much the mooncalf to escape his notice."

Arabella snatched up a fan and began to cool her heated cheeks with an agitated movement. "Your mama has many admirers, which is her due as one of the most beautiful hostesses in the ton."

"There is only the one who is constant, although I daresay that is because no one else can hold a candle to

Lord Carisbrooke. He is a true Corinthian, a nonesuch, and I do believe he is riding in the Park with her now," the girl added slyly, and Arabella jumped to her feet.

"Won't Miss Byford be looking for you?"

"I doubt it. She has taken a fancy to one of the footmen—not that I am supposed to know—and she is always glad of an opportunity to spoon with him. She won't miss me. No one ever does." She glanced at Arabella's gown and offered, "I have a blue sash you could borrow if you wish."

Her cousin's green eyes grew warm. "Oh, could I?"

Once again the child's face took on a sly look. "Only if you lend me *Prisoner of Desire*—just for tonight."

"That's outrageous!"

"Nevertheless, those are my terms."

"You're a monster."

"Mama calls me a cuckoo. She says she can't understand how she managed to produce such a plain child."

Arabella gasped. While it was true Molly favored her father, possessing a similarly lengthy nose and prominent chin, it seemed incomprehensible that a mother could have such a jaundiced opinion of her own child. "Your mama wouldn't be so cruel."

"I heard her say it to Papa as I passed her boudoir one day."

"Let that be a lesson to you, Molly: eavesdroppers never hear well of themselves."

"Do you want the sash or not?"

Arabella hesitated before going to the table, setting her wire-rimmed spectacles to one side and handing the girl the book. "Do not on any account allow your mama or Miss Byford to see it, and you must return it to me first thing tomorrow morning."

"Mama will be far too busy to notice my choice of

4

reading matter and so will Miss Byford," Molly answered as she skipped toward the door.

As it closed behind her, Arabella murmured, "You are more like your mama than you know."

Kitty Polstead greedily devoured every word written on the note that had accompanied an extravagant basket of flowers delivered to her late that afternoon. She absorbed into her memory each loving word it contained, and when she looked up, she was smiling. Her cornflower blue eyes, so much admired by the gentlemen of the ton, sparkled in the sunlight flooding through the second-floor window. Her honey blond hair, already dressed for the evening, was piled high on her head, with ringlets hanging over her ears and framing a face eulogized by male and female acquaintances alike.

As she clutched the precious note to her bosom she examined her reflection, satisfied with what she saw in the mirror. A peach-bloom complexion, full lips, and a pert nose combined to make her an acknowledged beauty. Only a lack of money had prevented her having a Season of her own, and she had been introduced to Sir Andrew Polstead at a neighbor's soiree. Immediately enchanted by her youth and beauty, the wealthy bachelor had swiftly married Kitty and brought her to London to preside over his large house in Berkeley Square.

The new Lady Polstead had taken the ton by storm, establishing herself as a great hostess in her first Season. Now as she gazed at her reflection in the mirror, admiring her own impeccable appearance—maintained by Dr. Manfred's exceedingly expensive Oil of Amaranthe—she felt invincible. No more poor Kitty Halstead, she now possessed everything she had ever wanted, including a devoted lover, a man pursued by many, who wanted no one but her. Life could not be sweeter.

When someone knocked at her boudoir door, she quickly pushed the note into the pocket of her peignoir just as her husband burst into the room. In truth, she wished only to ponder further on Lord Carisbrooke's complimentary words, and her husband was the last person she wanted to see.

"Andrew," she greeted him in her breathless voice, forcing a smile to her lips. "You look to be in something of a pucker, my dear."

"And well I might be! I have just been studying this month's bills and vouchers. Really, Kitty, you are growing ever more extravagant in your expenditure."

Her eyes grew wide. "It isn't as if you can't afford my little luxuries," she told him, her tone teasing.

"Haberdashers, linen-drapers, milliners, mantua-makers, gaming vowels, a Dr. Manfred . . ." He frowned suddenly. "You are not indisposed are you, Kitty?"

"If I am, I shall endeavor to have an *in*expensive illness."

His face creased into a fond smile. "Now, there is no need for sarcasm."

"I do it as much for you as anyone," she pouted. "I want you to be proud of me, Andrew."

"I am. Oh, indeed, I am, my dear."

"You must understand that our position in Society is costly to maintain, and then there's Molly. She is forever growing out of her clothes—not to mention Arabella."

"Arabella! I haven't noted your cousin dressed in the high crack of fashion."

All at once Sir Andrew's frown reappeared when he caught sight of the flowers, and he asked in outraged tones, "Is that one of Carisbrooke's extravagances?"

Lady Polstead appeared bewildered. "Oh no," she answered with an embarrassed laugh, her hand closing over the note safely hidden in her pocket. "The Devonshires sent it because they are unable to attend my ball tonight. Poor, dear Georgiana is under the weather."

Sir Andrew looked slightly less aggrieved. "I don't suppose *Carisbrooke* is likely to be indisposed."

His wife laughed uneasily. "I think his lordship is always in the peak of good health." As she spoke, she couldn't hide the note of pride that pervaded her voice when she spoke of her admirer.

"While we are on the subject and I have your undivided attention for once, I am bound to tell you, my dear, I don't much care for him always dancing attendance on you. Even Byron is more discreet in his pursuit of Caro Lamb."

Lady Polstead's laugh rang out in bell-like tones in an effort to disguise her unease. "I do trust you are not comparing me with that zany."

"Indeed, I do not!" Sir Andrew spluttered. "Didn't mean to do so, I assure you, my dear, but you must take my meaning."

"Don't trouble your head over Carisbrooke," his wife crooned soothingly. "He pays me no more attention than anyone else, I fancy."

"Balderdash! He's always pouring the butterboat over you, and I'd rather he didn't in so obvious a manner."

"Shall I tell him so?"

"I am telling *you*."

"Does this mean you are jealous, Andrew?" she teased.

"Not in the least!"

"Well, I like to believe you are. It is most flattering after all these years of marriage."

She moved closer to him and flicked a speck of snuff from his coat while silently musing that Weston's fine tailoring didn't sit as well on his shoulders as it did on Lucian Carisbrooke's.

Resolutely putting all thoughts of the marquess out of

her mind, she smiled flirtatiously at her husband. "I can be sure of your affection when I hear you voice such sentiments, especially when so many fetching females throw the handkerchief in your direction."

His smile was bashful. "I cannot conceive who you're thinking of, but you know I see only one woman wherever I go."

"Oh, you are such a romantic, Andrew. How could any other man possibly compare?"

He enfolded her in his arms with such vigor, she winced, but he was unaware of it. After a moment she drew away, saying, "Really, Andrew, we must make ourselves ready for the ball. It wouldn't do to be late for our own diversion. Everyone says it's likely to be the most talked-about event of the Season."

Looking disappointed, Sir Andrew pulled away. "Knowing you, my dear, I wouldn't expect anything less."

When he had gone, his wife drew a sigh of relief before she hurried to ring for her maidservant.

Chapter Two

$\mathcal{E}$very room in Polstead house was filled with a constantly changing vista of myriad colors as extravagantly gowned and jeweled ladies paraded through the crowded salons. The noise was almost deafening, with the excited guests laughing and conversing as if this was the very last night they could do so.

Arabella had yet to clap eyes on her cousin, but even so she knew Kitty would look the finest of them all. Wearing her own white lutestring gown, Arabella felt slightly self-conscious, but few people cast her more than a disinterested glance. Molly's satin sash fitted snugly around her tiny waist, and Arabella was aware, when she glanced into one of the many mirrors adorning the walls, reflecting the hundreds of candles burning brightly in their sconces, that she looked far younger than her three and twenty years.

As she approached the ballroom, Sir Andrew caught sight of her and called, "Bella, how fetching you look! You always have the knack of setting yourself apart from the throng."

She smiled wryly. He was quite ignorant of fashion, and would not be aware that the gown she wore was out of necessity and not choice. "Thank you, Andrew. You're very kind to say so."

"Not kind. Truthful. What is more, my dear, you

9

always sport a pretty toe, so you must reserve a cotillion for me later. I insist upon it!"

"It will be my pleasure."

He greeted another guest, and she passed into the ballroom. The vast salon was already crammed with the most influential people in the beau monde. As she searched the tightly packed crowd for a familiar face, she was squeezed and buffeted from all sides. When she stepped out of the way to allow one dandy to pass, she found herself squarely in the way of no less a personage than Lord Carisbrooke.

She drew a sharp breath, aware that he appeared irritated by finding so insignificant a creature in his way. His stare was quite truculent, almost demanding in its ferocity that she should remove herself from his path. Then, when she dropped a slight curtsy, he glanced past her as if she didn't even exist, which, although she considered herself inured to slights, was nevertheless hurtful. When she eventually contrived to move out of his way, he swept past her with scarcely a nod. Arabella watched him until he was swallowed up by the crowd, and hers was not the only admiring glance that followed his progress.

The incident, as trivial as it seemed, remained in her mind for a long while afterward, the memory of his dark, brooding stare staying with her, sending shivers down her spine. Sometime later, when she found herself close to the dance floor, where a number of people were assembled for a country-dance, she spotted her cousin at last. She was wearing a pale blue, high-waisted gown with a deep décolleté. The gown shimmered with crystal beads every time she moved, and the renowned Polstead sapphires nestled against her skin and in her hair. She looked utterly ravishing, and Arabella experienced a frisson of pride that this exotic creature was her relative.

Whereas she and Kitty shared similar coloring, they were quite unalike in every other way. It wasn't as if Arabella was strictly plain, only that next to Kitty Polstead, she paled to anonymity.

As was typical at such gatherings, Lady Polstead was surrounded by a group of acolytes all eager for a word from her lips or a mere smile. Kitty was invariably the center of a lively crowd at any function she attended. Some of Arabella's feeling of pleasure evaporated when she spied Lord Carisbrooke included in the admirers at her cousin's side.

Lucian Carisbrooke. Lucifer to those who failed to find favor with the nonpareil, and few did. The most handsome man alive, Molly had called him. Arabella couldn't be so categoric, but he was positively the most well-favored gentleman she had ever clapped eyes upon.

His immaculate evening clothes, the perfectly folded neck cloth, complemented his dark coloring as well as Kitty's sapphires did hers. His brown curls were combed into a Brutus style and his lips, as he gazed down at the woman by his side, were formed into a satyr's smile. High cheekbones gave him a look of hauteur that only added to his magnetism, and he was said to be a master of all the Corinthian arts. Arabella wondered what it would be like to be courted by such a man, and then hastily dismissed the treacherous thought from her mind.

"So serious!" she heard someone chide, and turning on her heel, she snapped out of her grave reflections to discover Lord Redesby at her side.

He was a complete contrast to the gentleman previously occupying her thoughts. The baron was an elderly gentleman, more of a dandy with an excessive, rather than aesthetic, taste in clothes. But he invariably sought her out when she was ignored by all her cousin's other acquaintances, and she could only be grateful for his condescension.

She rewarded him with a smile.

"Ah, that is much better. Now, would you do me the very great honor of standing up with me, Miss Trentham?"

"It will be a pleasure," she answered wholeheartedly.

He escorted her into the set, and she was relieved to note that Kitty was leading it with Andrew. Lord Carisbrooke was partnering the rather fearsome Lady Brimston, held in awe by so many, but she appeared to pose no problem for him. He was engaging her with his most charming manner, and the haughty matron, who instilled fear even into Kitty's heart, was actually responding to him in a skittish way.

"You look more fetching when you smile," Lord Redesby was telling her, and Arabella gave him her attention again, feeling guilty at attending Lord Carisbrooke too closely and for too long.

"Yes, I daresay I do, but it's not the easiest task in such a crush."

After the dance was over, Arabella indulged in a little idle chatter with some of the chaperons and wallflowers with whom she usually spent much of her time at such functions. On this occasion, though, the congenial conversation did not hold her attention. She felt unaccountably unsettled and attempted unsuccessfully to pinpoint the actual source of her discomfiture. Eventually she excused herself to wander around, marveling at the extravagant fashions and sparkling jewelry worn by the ladies. Many of the gentlemen were equally splendid, in their uniform black or dark blue evening coats contrasting vividly with the stark white of their shirts and neck cloths. Some of the gentlemen guests wore colorful military or naval uniforms enhanced by trim figures owed to frequent visits to Gentleman Jackson's Salon.

Arabella had seen Lord Carisbrooke leaving that temple of health and fitness when she'd been running errands for Kitty in Bond Street one day. She'd paused to cast him a hopeful glance, but he haughtily strode right past her without a glimmer of recognition and climbed up onto the box of his waiting curricle.

The ball was quite, quite wonderful, she told herself as she glanced around, still unused to all the splendor of an evening with the *haute ton*.

"Bella, you're the only person apart from ape leaders and chaperons who isn't wearing blue!" Kitty remonstrated when she came upon her cousin in the midst of a throng. "You really must learn to conform, you know."

"I don't possess a blue gown," Arabella sought to explain, but she was too late, for Kitty was already being whisked away by an admirer to dance the new sensation, the waltz.

A little while later, when seeking out a familiar face, she heard a shrill voice declare, "It is too bad! The most eligible bachelor in London, and he is head over heels in love with Lady Polstead. It's the most vexing situation I have ever had the misfortune to encounter!"

"You can't say you haven't tried to attract his attention, making sheep's eyes at him at every opportunity," her companion answered.

Arabella turned to note it was two pretty debutantes who were discussing Kitty. She couldn't blame them their envy. The attentiveness of the marquess was in itself a prize for any young lady. Unfortunately for all those on the catch for a husband, he was never far from her cousin's side. It gave Arabella no pleasure to admit he was passionately enamored of Kitty.

"You shouldn't appear so eager to court his favor, Hattie," the young lady counseled. "You're always

13

throwing the handkerchief—to no avail. He doesn't even acknowledge you're alive!"

"He would if he wasn't already infatuated with Kitty Polstead. It really isn't fair. She possesses an adoring husband, and now she's closer than an inkle weaver with Lord Carisbrooke. She might be deemed a beauty, but it's not as if she's remotely *young*."

Arabella had heard enough, and made her way out of the room. Even after six months in London, she still felt alien when faced with the gossip and intrigue that ensued at every gathering of the beau monde. When she first arrived at Polstead House, she had expected to take a greater part in social affairs, but it soon became clear Kitty had neither the time nor the inclination to introduce her young relative into Society. In truth, Arabella was grateful enough to be given a congenial home and to have the opportunity to be with Molly as she grew up.

No one would notice she had left the ball, Arabella thought as she walked away from the public apartments, down a corridor that was both quiet and cool. No one was likely to miss her if she went back to her room to read the delightful book she had borrowed only that day from the circulating library in Bond Street. It was lucky Molly hadn't spotted that one, for it was much more lurid than *Prisoner of Desire*.

Suddenly she came to an abrupt halt when she caught sight of the unmistakable figures of Lord Carisbrooke and her cousin farther down the corridor. They were quite unaware of her presence and probably wouldn't have noticed her even if she had moved nearer, so intent were they on each other. Their heads were close together, one fair and one dark, so well matched. Their voices were low as they conversed with great seriousness. The appearance of intimacy was so notable, Arabella's heart lurched with dismay. To go forward, as she needed to do

14

in order to reach her room, would be embarrassing to all of them, so without making a sound she turned on her heel and returned the way she had come, in the hope of reaching the servants' stairs at the other end of the house.

The first familiar face she encountered as she approached the ballroom was Sir Andrew, who had every appearance of a man in high dudgeon. "Arabella!" he exclaimed. "Have you seen my wife at all?"

She hesitated before she replied, quite truthfully, "I saw her a short while ago with Lady Macintyre."

"I can't find her anywhere! Neglecting our guests is quite inexcusable."

Arabella slipped her arm into his and guided him back into the ballroom. "Kitty is a wonderful hostess, as anyone will attest, Andrew. By the by, the master of ceremonies has just announced a cotillion, and you did promise . . ."

As he led her into the set, she glanced toward the door, relieved to observe the errant couple return to the ballroom and move in separate directions. She sighed, however, for she feared their attachment was attracting too much attention. The couple's passion was rendering them careless. It was only a matter of time before a public scandal, like that of Lord Byron and Lady Caroline Lamb, ensued. That was something which didn't bear contemplating, for Sir Andrew was already both jealous and suspicious.

She sighed again before turning to her partner and bestowing on him a smile that belied her disquiet.

Chapter Three

"*I*'ll wager you're too old to catch me!" Molly taunted as she raced out of Arabella's bedchamber and into the corridor.

"You odious child, bring that book back here to me!" her cousin responded with a laugh before proceeding to chase after her, as was intended.

Molly paused at the head of the curved flight of stairs leading to a massive hall, to make certain she was being followed, and then she chuckled before she ran down.

"Molly!" Arabella cried in mock exasperation as she sped after her.

By the time she had reached the landing, there was no sign of the child anywhere to be seen, and she hurried down the marble steps in pursuit of her. She'd almost reached the bottom when her satin slipper caught in the hem of her chintz gown. Gasping with shock, she pitched forward, unable to prevent herself crashing down hard onto the tessellated floor.

Suddenly, in the split second she anticipated the painful landing, she was pulled upright against a broad chest by a pair of strong hands. Arabella had no time to recover from her fright before she found herself on eye level with the first cape of a broadcloth driving coat. She looked up abruptly, past an all too familiar square jaw, the sensuous lips that haunted her dreams, and nostrils flaring with outrage, to meet a pair of eyes, the color of steel. The moment she recognized the unmistakable features of Lord Carisbrooke, she drew back. Her heart was thudding against her ribs, something she attributed to her near fall.

"One child is outside of enough," he declared.

Aware that her hair had worked loose from its pins and was now cascading untidily about her ears, she pulled back even further, and her cheeks immediately flooded with color.

"Bella isn't a child." Molly chuckled when she revealed herself at last from behind a life-size statue of Zeus.

"Beg pardon," the marquess replied from his lofty height. "I see now your nursemaid isn't quite as young as I first thought, but certainly not old enough to generate discipline in you."

The color in Arabella's cheeks grew deeper when Molly began to chuckle even louder. "This is my cousin, Miss Trentham."

Arabella averted her eyes from his, and mumbled, "I am obliged to you for your assistance, my lord. It warms my heart to know you would come to the aid of a mere servant."

His face took on a look of affront, but Arabella was heedless of any consequences that might ensue from her impudence. He might be bang up to the mark in all things, but in her opinion he was far too starched for his own good.

"What on earth is going on?" an imperious voice demanded to know, and everyone looked up to where Lady Polstead was waiting on the top step.

She couldn't fail to be aware of the picture she presented, standing there in so prominent a position for all of them to see. Her royal blue velvet pelisse, frogged and trimmed with fox fur, and a military-style shako atop her honey-colored curls suited her to perfection. With one hand tucked into a matching muff and the other lightly resting on the banister rail, she was a vision of beauty.

"I am being somewhat diverted by your daughter and cousin," the marquess replied, sounding bored.

"I wonder you dared to show yourselves. You look disgusting," Lady Polstead snapped. "Both of you be pleased to remove yourself from my sight."

Then she came slowly down the stairs, subjecting Arabella to a cold stare, and none of them could fail to be aware that Lord Carisbrooke was intent upon her every movement.

"I trusted you with my daughter. I intend her to grow up as a lady, not a hoyden."

"I do beg your pardon most heartily," Arabella stammered, glancing uneasily at the marquess, whose attention was still fixed upon Kitty.

"We were only playing, Mama," Molly told her in a plaintive voice.

"Do as you are bid!"

"Can't I come with you in Lord Carisbrooke's chariot, Mama?"

"Don't be ridiculous, child. Go away and attend your appearance and your lessons. Whatever will you want next, I wonder?"

"No need to be such a crosspatch," the marquess gently chided, his manner transformed so completely, Arabella felt all the more disgruntled. "They're both very young."

"Indeed," Lady Polstead agreed as she moved toward the door and rounded on him with a dazzling smile. "You can have no notion how difficult it is to raise a young lady."

"I'm sure you have no cause for concern," he assured

18

her in emollient tones. "Miss Polstead has a wonderful mother to emulate."

Kitty visibly preened at such praise, but her eyes grew cold when they alighted upon Arabella. Then she linked her arm into that of her companion. Arabella sketched a curtsy to Lord Carisbrooke, who nodded briefly in her direction, his attention wholly centered upon Lady Polstead.

The two young ladies watched them go and as the marquess assisted Lady Polstead onto the box of his high-perch phaeton, Arabella was sure they were already oblivious to everyone else.

Lord Carisbrooke drove away displaying enviable panache, his companion's bad humor already gone. Molly sighed and said wistfully, "So divine. They're gone to ride in the Park. I do so wish I could go with them."

"Why don't we go out too?" Arabella suggested.

"To the Park?" the child asked hopefully.

"I have a better notion: we'll go to the menagerie at the Tower to see all the strange and exotic animals. How would you like that?"

Molly began to jump up and down with delight, and Arabella was glad that her mother's disposition had not depressed her spirits too greatly.

"Your mama is correct about our appearance," she added. "We will need to change our clothes first."

She held out her hand to her young cousin, who chuckled while they ran up the stairs together.

"I had no notion you had so youthful a cousin residing with you," Lord Carisbrooke admitted the following afternoon.

"That tiresome girl." Lady Polstead sighed.

"I fully understand your feelings on that score. I gained the distinct impression she's an impertinent chit."

"You wouldn't believe what I am obliged to endure on account of that girl."

"Why on earth do you tolerate her presence?" he asked as he toyed with a lock of her hair.

"When her father died about six months ago, Bella was left in somewhat straightened circumstances, and I felt it only right to offer her a home with us."

"That was very good of you, my love."

She smiled. "Truth to tell, Luce, it was Andrew's suggestion, and she does have her uses. She's a green goose, but she has taken a liking to Molly and is very good with her. I suppose that's because she's no more than a child herself. Her presence gives me more time to be with you, and that is one good reason to endure her in my house." She snuggled closer to him on the chaise longue. "I do so appreciate any opportunity to be alone with you— entirely alone, that is. I only wish we could always be together like this."

In a carefully studied tone, he answered, "We could be together forevermore—if you truly wished it, Kitty."

"How is that possible, my dear? I'm a married woman." She tossed back her head in a theatrical fashion intended to show to advantage the long line of her neck. "Oh, how bitterly aware I am of that. If only I'd met you before Polstead."

He sat up and looked at her keenly, causing her to raise her hand to stroke his cheek. "Well, you didn't, but we could always put that matter to rights by running away together."

Kitty Polstead swung her legs over the side of the chaise and sat up straight. "Don't tease me, Luce. It's impossible and you know it."

The marquess jumped to his feet. "Why? Why is it

impossible? The most important thing is for us to be together, and that would be the only way."

"Think of our respective positions in Society!"

"To the devil with that! If it means we are forever damned from being together, I'd as lief give it all up."

She stared at him in astonishment. "I have never heard you speak so rashly before and, in my opinion, without true thought or consideration. Where on earth would we go?"

"Now the war is over, we could run off to Paris. I'm not without means, Kitty. We'd be able to live in great fashion in the most stylish place on earth."

"I've worked too long and too hard to reach the position I'm in to give it all up now. There'd be a horrible scandal. I'd be an outcast from all my friends, just like Caro Lamb. You ask too much of me."

The marquess thumped his clenched fist down on the top of a bureau. "Dash it all! What is more important to you? Your situation in Society, or our feelings for each other?"

She went up to him, putting her hands on his unrelenting shoulders and pressed her cheek against his back. "You know full well the answer to that, but I do have my child to think about too."

His laugh was a hollow one. "If that is so, this must be the very first time she has taken precedence in your considerations."

She withdrew from him. "This new mood of yours is alarming to me, Lucian."

"Good. Now perhaps you will take me seriously." He turned to face her, and she couldn't be in any doubt about his resolve.

"If I left Polstead, he wouldn't allow me to have my child."

"I'll help you fight for her."

"It would be to no avail. He has powerful friends."

"So have I, Kitty. So have I."

She put one hand to her disordered curls and then drew her shawl more closely about her. "This is all very sudden. We both have so much to lose."

"And to gain."

"Even so you'll be obliged to give me some time to consider."

He reached out and caught her wrist in a vice-like grip, drawing her back toward him. "I am not accustomed to sharing females with another man."

"That gentleman is my husband."

"There is no need to remind me, but the time has come for you to choose between us." His face took on an intensity of expression that both thrilled and frightened her. "I want you more than any woman I have ever encountered, and I mean to have you whatever the cost. I don't intend to go on forever taking crumbs from Sir Andrew Polstead's table."

Kitty Polstead shivered with delight, and when he lowered his head and claimed her lips in a passionate kiss, she responded wholeheartedly before he abruptly drew away.

"You're like a fire in my blood, Kitty. I must have you, and I know you feel the same way about me. Go now and think on what I have said, but don't take long about it. I'm impatient to be with you and to show the world you're mine."

Appearing shaken, she nodded. "I will, naturally, give your proposal my earnest consideration."

"You do want me as much as I want you, Kitty?" he asked with uncharacteristic uncertainty.

She pressed herself against him. "Oh, never doubt it, my love. You mean everything to me."

"Then, there can be nothing else to think over."

He held her against him, kissing her with a new desperation that inflamed her as never before. That this most eligible gentleman favored her above all others who vied for his affection was heady enough, but knowing he was actually willing to give up everything for her sake was even more exciting. His wish to elope was worrying, though. She had no notion what she would do about it, but for now she wanted nothing more than to enjoy the pleasures only he was capable of bestowing on her. The rest would wait for another day.

Chapter Four

*A*rabella entered her cousin's boudoir with great trepidation. Over the last few days Kitty Polstead's mood had been volatile, even by her own standards, and she and Molly knew from past experience it was best to avoid her whenever possible.

Her ladyship was reclining on a daybed, a vinaigrette clutched in her hand. She wore a peignoir trimmed with swansdown and even in dishabille she never failed to look less than exquisite.

"Kitty, you sent for me . . ."

She raised her head and waved Arabella into the room. "Be sure to close the door behind you. There are no servants lurking in the hall, are there?"

"No one," her cousin reassured her.

"Andrew?"

"He has not arrived home yet. Kitty, if this is about the other day . . ." Her cousin frowned, and Arabella went on, "In the hall with Molly and Lord Carisbrooke."

The other woman waved her hand dismissively. "Oh, that. Indeed not."

Arabella experienced a measure of relief, but still discerned a problem. "Is something amiss, Kitty? You look all done up."

"Oh yes. Everything is wrong. I find myself in a terrible coil." She looked up, and Arabella couldn't fail to be aware of the despair in the woman's eyes. "Can I rely upon your discretion, my dear?"

"Naturally."

"I need your help. It's imperative I get a note to Lord Carisbrooke—and the matter is of the greatest delicacy."

Arabella drew back as if stung. "Doesn't your abigail usually deliver your billets-doux?"

"This is no time to stand on points! It is not a love letter, and Temple is indisposed. There is no one else I can trust to do this! I don't want to put too fine a point on it, Bella, but this is a matter of the utmost import."

Arabella drew a sigh and pulled a stool up to the daybed. "Have you and his lordship parted brass rags, Kitty?"

Lady Polstead laid her head back and laughed brokenly. "No. Not yet, at least."

"Then, what . . . ?"

"Oh, Bella, I am in such torment. He insists I elope with him to Paris."

Her cousin was aghast. "Kitty, you can't!"

Again Lady Polstead laughed. "No, indeed I cannot, but he has been importuning me to do so for days, and now he has sent me an ultimatum." She snatched up a note from a nearby table. "He says he won't allow me to shilly-shally any longer. Those are his very words! I am to meet him at the end of Park Street at four-thirty this evening, where he'll be waiting with a traveling carriage. He insists I come with nothing more than a cloak bag, and he will purchase for me all I need when we arrive in Paris. A cloak bag! As if that would suffice for even the one night!"

Arabella's glance strayed to the mantel clock. "Fourthirty! That is in less than half an hour."

"He has obviously taken leave of his senses, evidently

25

unhinged by love for me, but in this mood of desperation he could do me much damage."

It was embarrassing for Arabella to hear these declarations. Indeed, she couldn't envisage the marquess, divine as he was, making such romantic pronouncements, and for all her apparent alarm, she had an inkling Kitty was rather enjoying the drama. All at once Arabella felt a fleeting pity for Lord Carisbrooke, who had always appeared invulnerable. The most eligible bachelor in the ton was about to be horribly humiliated, and she didn't want to be a witness to it.

"You don't intend to go?" she asked, all at once fearful.

"No, I cannot. Polstead and I are engaged to dine at Devonshire House this evening. How could I possibly cry off the Devonshires? That is why I require you to deliver the note—without any further delay. It will break my heart to wound him in this manner, and he will be distempered for a short while, but my decision is made."

"How did you get into this coil, Kitty?"

Lady Polstead's eyes narrowed. "Don't pretend you wouldn't have acted in the very same manner given the opportunity."

Confused, Arabella looked away.

"He's so charming and handsome, and everyone envies me his attention," Lady Polstead continued. "I vow to you I didn't intend the matter to go this far. I never thought it was more than an innocent flirtation." As Arabella cast her a disbelieving look, her cousin went on, "You will do this for me, won't you, Bella?"

She stared imploringly at Arabella, who continued to hesitate. "You owe it to me, Bella. I have been good to you."

Arabella drew a sigh and nodded. "I shall go directly and fetch my bonnet and pelisse."

Before she had a chance to stand up, her cousin jumped to her feet. "There is no time for that. Take my cloak and do *hurry*."

She tossed a cloak trimmed with sable onto Arabella's shoulders, and then pressed a note into her hands before rushing her toward the door. "Hurry, now," she repeated. "If no one appears at the appointed time, he is very like to come here, and that would be disastrous."

When Arabella reached the landing, she came face-to-face with Molly, who said, "Why are *you* wearing Mama's new cloak?"

"I'm just going out on an errand for her, and it cannot wait."

The child's eyes narrowed. "What kind of errand?"

Arabella sighed again, this time with frustration. Then she brushed past Molly, murmuring, "I'll join you for supper when I return."

Only when she reached the square did she question the sense of what she was doing. She owed the roof over her head to Sir Andrew's good offices, and if he were to discover her acting as a go-between for Kitty and her admirer, she might well end up homeless and destitute. On the other hand, she reasoned, Kitty had decided to end the attachment and that could only be to the good. The assistance she was about to render her cousin would benefit Sir Andrew too. In any event, she had no time to waste on pondering the rights and wrongs of the situation, and she hurried on.

As she turned the corner, sure enough a closed carriage was standing at the curb. Unlike Lord Carisbrooke's escutcheoned high-perch phaeton and racing curricle—often to be seen parked outside Polstead House—this one did not bear any identifying marks. When she was closer to the carriage, she slowed her pace, all at once nervous. Lord Carisbrooke always appeared so formidable to her.

He was accustomed to having his own way in all things. Females dangled for the briefest word from his lips. Being jilted by the one woman he desired above all others was going to be a profound blow to his considerable pride, and Arabella did not relish being witness to it. She hoped he wouldn't make her the target for his disappointment and vent his wrath on her.

When the bells of St. Margaret's Church rang out, she pressed on, taking a deep breath as she approached the carriage. Just as she drew abreast of the vehicle, a waiting footman flung open the door, a hand emerged from inside and pulled her into it.

"I thought you'd decided not to come," the marquess told her. Then to the driver as the carriage sprung forward, "Don't spare the horses, Windle!"

Arabella fell back into the squabs, gasping in alarm. As she did so the hood of the cloak dropped back, revealing her identity.

Lord Carisbrooke's smile of welcome faded, and he sat forward as the carriage thundered down the street. "You! Where is Lady Polstead?"

"That is what I am here to tell you. She isn't coming." A strange, frightening expression came over his face. "I brought you her note."

She held it out to him with a trembling hand, and he snatched it from her. "Please . . . stop the carriage while you read it, my lord."

She was sure he didn't hear her plea as he read the brief note, his face suffusing with color with every word. "Perfidious jade!" he exclaimed, crushing the parchment in his fist with a strength and ferocity that made Arabella flinch.

"My lord—"

"Be silent!" he roared, and she once more sank into the squabs while he stared fiercely out of the window, his chin resting on his clenched fist as the familiar well-ordered streets and squares faded into the distance.

"She is a married woman," Arabella ventured to point out after a brief silence, and he turned his tortured gaze on her once again.

"Married but ill-used, and desperately unhappy. It is only natural to wish to save her from such misery."

She understood at last his motivation. Kitty had used the pretense of an unhappy marriage to inspire his sense of chivalry.

"I suppose," he went on, "she only remained with Sir Andrew for her daughter's sake."

Arabella's only response was to ask timidly, "Could we not turn around now? My cousin will be concerned about my disappearance if I don't return to the house shortly."

He smiled at last, but it was merely a cruel curve of his lips. "Do you truly believe she will trouble herself for anything other than her own pleasures?"

She averted her eyes from his cold gray gaze. "Even so I should like to go back."

"Am I such a terrible cove that you too wish to rid yourself of my company?"

"You are all any woman could wish for, my lord, but not when you are in this present mood, and certainly not in these circumstances." He looked surprised and then even more so when she added, "Do you realize you are in effect abducting me?"

"I confess I did not until you were good enough to inform me of the fact. It is possibly the most exciting thing that has ever happened to you in all your miserable life."

Angry, Arabella retorted, "My life is certainly not miserable! I am well content with my lot."

"Then, you must be an utter fool," he answered sarcastically, something that made her even more angry.

"At least I am gratified that my cousin has come to her senses. How she could possibly allow herself to become attached to someone as proud and disagreeable as you is beyond all understanding."

"You couldn't comprehend the feelings of someone as passionate as Kitty Polstead. I doubt if you would ever have the opportunity of enjoying the company of any gentleman beyond the walls of Bedlam."

Arabella gasped. "I had no notion rudeness was another of your failings."

"It was you who called me proud and disagreeable."

"And so you are!" she insisted, aware that her face had become very red. "And in not allowing me to return immediately, you are behaving in an entirely odious manner that I would not have equated with a gentleman."

"I agree, but I am justified for any lapse in propriety. Your cousin has flirted with me, led me on, and now has made me appear a fool in front of the entire ton. I believe I am fully entitled to feel aggrieved."

"You knew she was a married lady with a child when you first made her acquaintance."

"Your cousin doesn't give a fig for either her husband, who ill-uses her, or her child." He leaned forward, and his demeanor was so irate she shrank away, her own outrage cowed immediately. "There is nothing to stop me having my revenge on *you*. No one to prevent me from ravishing you on the floor of this carriage and then abandoning you on the wayside."

He truly alarmed her. And she didn't doubt in his present mood, he was capable of all manner of outrages. Still, she found sufficient courage to counter, "To what purpose, my lord? As you so rightly said, Kitty will not care what becomes of me."

30

To her surprise, he looked away from her. "You needn't fear me, madam. I am not so distempered I need take a green girl for my pleasures. Disappointment, however, is making me peevish." Arabella experienced a modicum of relief, although she still remained alert. "I'm beginning to feel sharp-set," he went on a moment later. "Windle, stop at the next inn we come to."

"This is not the best area to stop, my lord," came the coachman's reply.

"I have no intention of allowing Miss . . ." He cast her an irritated look. "What the devil is your name?" Her lips formed into a rebellious line. "Speak up, madam. There is no one here to betray your secret."

"Trentham. Arabella Trentham."

"I cannot allow Miss Trentham or myself to go hungry just because the hostelries in this part of the country aren't bang up to the mark. We'll have to put up with something less prime."

"Very well, my lord," came the resigned reply from the box.

"Let us hope the inn has a post chaise to take me back to London, although you'll be obliged to stand the damage. I have no money with me."

The marquess smiled without mirth. "It's very admirable of you to want to report back to your cousin."

"Kitty won't be at home. She and Sir Andrew are to dine with the Devonshires this evening."

"*I* had an invitation to that hurricane," he told her in outraged tones.

When the carriage began to slow down, the marquess put his head briefly out of the window. "There's an inn ahead of us. Stop there, Windle!"

"Thank goodness." Arabella sighed. "I shall be able to get back before anyone misses me."

"If you never arrived back, would Lady Polstead

notice you were gone until she had a disagreeable task for you to undertake?"

Arabella's eyes narrowed. "How can you make such horrid remarks about a lady you profess to adore?"

"The woman I thought I loved does not exist, Miss. . . ."

"Trentham," she snapped, "Arabella Trentham."

Chapter Five

The carriage clattered into the yard, and the moment it came to a halt, the footman jumped down, lowered the steps, and then opened the door. The marquess climbed down first before he offered his hand to Arabella, who hesitated before accepting his assistance, although she was quick to withdraw her hand from his at the earliest possible moment.

He subjected her to a ferocious stare before he glanced at his surroundings. With some considerable difficulty, Arabella tore her equally truculent gaze from his, and each viewed the ramshackle establishment with dismay, for it was immediately obvious that this was no post house and an alternative mode of transport was not likely to be available.

The inn's sign creaked on rusty hinges above their heads. "What is this place?" his lordship asked of no one in particular, his irritation appearing to heighten.

"You did insist on your coachman stopping," Arabella reminded him.

"If it's your habit to make inane remarks of that nature, it is no wonder your cousin regards you as tiresome."

"I daresay she now regards you in a similar light," she snapped.

He cast her an icy look before he glanced up at the sign

33

once again. "The Jolly Hangman," he read in disbelief. "Good Lord!"

Despite the tension in the air between them, Arabella was hard-pressed to stifle her chuckles just as the innkeeper and an ostler came running into the yard.

"What will be your pleasure, sir?" the landlord asked, rubbing his hands together.

"That is altogether beyond your capabilities," the marquess replied in a bored tone. "In the meantime, I will settle for food and rest for my horses and servants, and dinner for me and my . . ."

He turned to stare at Arabella, suddenly aware of their invidious situation, and all at once bereft of words. Her eyes opened wide in alarm as the landlord continued to smile expectantly at them both.

"Sister," she blurted out. "My brother and I are on our way to visit our sick mother. An emergency, you understand."

The fellow smiled slyly. "I understand, perfectly, ma'am. The stable block is currently empty, sir, a rare, quiet time at the Jolly Hangman, so there's plenty of room for your horses and carriage. I wouldn't want so fine a vehicle to be left prey to the elements." He glanced appraisingly at Arabella in her sable-trimmed cloak. "You and your . . . er . . . sister, sir, will have the finest dinner my cook can provide, and the young lady a room in which to refresh herself."

The marquess tossed a coin at the fellow. "Get on the bustle, man. I don't want to die of hunger while you go on like a rattle."

The landlord bowed several times before the marquess brushed him aside and strode into the dingy building followed at a trot by the innkeeper and rather more reluctantly by Arabella. Once they were inside Lord Carisbrooke slowed sufficiently to allow her to catch up with

34

him and inclined his head toward her, saying, "That was quick-witted of you, Miss. . . ."

"Trentham, and posing as your sister might make it easier for you to remember my name. It's Arabella, but as Trentham seems beyond your memory, call me Bella when anyone else is listening."

While the landlord ushered the marquess into a private parlor, his sour-faced wife led Arabella up the stairs to a small bedchamber dominated by a half-tester bed that didn't look as if it had been slept in for years. The hangings and counterpane appeared none too clean, but it was no more than she would have expected from an establishment of this kind.

"We don't get the quality stopping here very often," the woman informed her. "We're way off the main highway. Where are you bound, then?" she went on to inquire.

Arabella turned on her heel, starting slightly. She stared at the woman for a few moments, much as she and Lord Carisbrooke had done to the landlord before answering breathlessly, "Leicester."

"It's a long way from here. Where do you come from, then?"

"London."

"I'm not so good with directions, miss, but I reckon you and the young sir are going in the wrong direction. We be south of London, we be."

Once again, Arabella's eyes opened wide with alarm. She recalled belatedly what Kitty had told her—they were bound for Paris! Dover! What a boner! She gave the woman a sheepish smile. "I thought Leominster *was* south of London."

"Leominster! I thought you said Leicester."

"Where is this place?"

"Bollerton."

Arabella was no wiser and persisted. "Where is Bollerton?"

"Five miles north of Tenterfield."

A young maidservant trundled up the stairs in their wake, carrying a pitcher of hot water, which she tipped into a bowl. She gaped unashamedly at Arabella, as if she were a rare and exotic animal.

"Come along, Grissel, let's leave the young lady to her ablutions," the innkeeper's wife told the maid.

After the two women had gone, Arabella went to the window to view the expanse of fields beyond the inn. In the distance she could see a church steeple and reckoned there must be a village not too far distant. She tried to open the window, and the casement creaked open beneath her hand. Peering down, she noted the ivy-covered walls and reckoned she could easily climb down, but to what end? Closing the window again, she sighed. With no wheeled transport and no notion where she was, she couldn't get far.

Although she would never own to it, even under the most dire pressure, she was vexed to acknowledge that the marquess had been quite correct in stating this was the most exciting thing that had ever happened to her. In fact, if she weren't constantly aware that Kitty was anxiously awaiting her report in London, Arabella could actually enjoy herself in a way. It was rather like situations arising in some of the novels she read so voraciously. In her cousin's absence, Lord Carisbrooke was angry with her, but for all his shocked bluster she was certain he meant her no harm, and would soon wish to return to London himself.

When she went down to the parlor, she found him staring into a hastily kindled fire. As it was evident the parlor was hardly ever used, the logs were damp and gave off little heat. When she entered the room, he turned in her direction, and she saw that he held a glass brimming with wine. He looked both handsome and dangerous as the struggling flames cast shadows across his dark face, and involuntarily her heart skipped a beat.

"I beg your pardon, for the ambience of this place," he told her abruptly before he downed the dark liquid and refilled the glass from a carafe on the table. "It isn't remotely what either of us are accustomed to."

He had removed his caped driving coat to reveal a buff-colored coat whose fine tailoring by Weston was unmistakable. His skintight pantaloons were without a wrinkle, and his neck cloth folded well enough to satisfy Beau Brummell himself.

Aware of too obvious a scrutiny, she averted her eyes and answered, "Luxurious living is very new to me, my lord, although I would doubt the wisdom of bringing my cousin to an establishment of this sort."

The moment the words were out, Arabella regretted them, for the mention of Kitty's name caused him pain and that was evident from his expression. "Perhaps it is just as well," she went on quickly, "so we are both reminded that such places exist."

He came toward her, saying, "I could easily live without the knowledge."

"Ah yes, I know. The poor must remain invisible."

It was a discomforting feeling allowing him to remove her cloak—Kitty's cloak. He pulled out a chair, and she sat down just as the landlord, his wife, and the maidservant entered, bearing various dishes that were set down on the table.

"My finest feast," the landlord announced with great pride as both the marquess and Arabella viewed the unappetizing food with dismay. First the maidservant and wife fled, then the proprietor stomped out of the room.

"Not a sight to set us on the scramble," his lordship

37

remarked as he surveyed the selection of overcooked and stringy meats and bread curling up at the edges. "I daresay it is better than nothing, Miss . . . er . . . Bella."

She remained perched primly on the edge of her chair. "No, I thank you."

"Come now. You must be hungry."

"Abduction has had the effect of spoiling my appetite, so be so kind as to excuse me."

He shrugged slightly and took a few morsels onto a plate before seating himself on the edge of the table, one booted leg swinging as he ate. "That is far too dramatic a construction on the matter. It was mistaken identity. You were wearing Kitty's cloak."

"A mistake easily rectified before we had gone fifty yards down the road."

"My anger isn't so easily appeased."

"That is none of my affair."

"I'm afraid your involvement makes it so."

"The innkeeper doesn't believe I am your sister," she announced resentfully.

"I didn't suppose he would, but as long as I pay him well, it won't trouble his sense of morality all that much."

"How arrogant of you to say so!" she protested.

"There are those who say arrogance is my finest quality."

"Indeed, I say it is a fault, and a grievous one at that."

"My, my, you are a pokerish little prig, aren't you. How does Kitty endure it?"

Hurt by his teasing, she replied, "Speaking of my cousin will not put either of us in a happy frame of mind. All that concerns me now is when I will be returned to Polstead House."

He paused while chewing on a chicken leg. Then he put the plate down, drained another glass of wine, and wiped his fingers thoroughly on a grubby napkin before subjecting her to the full force of his disturbing gaze. "Has her ladyship left you some chores to do while she dines with the Devonshires?" Arabella stiffened in the face of his sarcasm. "Is that what this anxiety to return is all about?"

"My true need is to escape your horrid company, my lord."

"Say that in the drawing rooms of the ton, and the tattle baskets would consider you had windmills in your head."

"We are not in the drawing rooms of the ton."

"You are probably never invited to any fashionable diversion. Do you enjoy being a skivvy?"

Arabella jumped to her feet, her eyes snapping with anger. "How dare you! What do you know about being poor? About being beholden to others for the very roof over your head?"

"Now, now, my dear, don't fly up into the boughs with me," he crooned. "It's your cousin you should reserve your anger for—she is the one who put you in this position."

"All I did was deliver her note to you and, in retrospect, if I were asked again, I would far rather risk being cast into the workhouse than have the remotest contact with you!"

"Do you always deliver her billets-doux?" he asked, his tone chilly now.

"You should know that task is usually entrusted to her abigail, but unfortunately for me Temple is indisposed, else you'd find yourself companion to a servant indulging in a fit of the vapors."

They continued to glare at each other until there came a knock on the door.

"I beg your pardon for the intrusion, my lord"—Arabella

recognized the voice of one of the footmen—"but the horses aren't fit to go on, and Windle reckons if we move on tonight we'll not get far."

"Hell and damnation!" the marquess said. Then in a calmer tone, he asked, "Is Windle in no doubt?"

"None at all, my lord, and I'm in full agreement with him."

"Well, there is little about cattle Windle doesn't know, although I am loath to remain in this doss house a moment longer than necessary. Just make absolutely certain the team's ready to leave first thing in the morning. Is that clear?"

Lord Carisbrooke slammed the door shut with such force, Arabella started nervously. "I absolutely refuse to stay all night under the same roof with you," she stammered.

"It appears we have no choice in the matter, and don't think for one moment I am happy with this turn of events, for it vexes me as much as you."

Arabella's eyes narrowed dangerously. "This is a ploy. You planned this, didn't you?"

The marquess removed his enameled snuffbox from the pocket of his coat and was about to take a pinch, when he paused to look at her in amazement. "Why would I do such a thing? For the pleasure of your company?" He returned the snuffbox to his pocket before adding, to her further chagrin, "I'm sure you can't be sufficiently cork-brained to harbor such a grand delusion. You are welcome to the bedchamber. I shall rack up in here."

Arabella didn't know whether to be relieved or insulted. "When we leave . . . I presume you do intend to return to London immediately."

The marquess nibbled thoughtfully on a piece of plum pie before turning on his heel to look at her again. "I'm hipped with London. I have it in mind that if I hadn't been so bored, I mightn't have found your cousin so entrancing."

"You are not the first to become a mooncalf."

"I'll warrant I'm the first to make such a cake of myself."

"You will send *me* back, won't you?"

"I've a mind not to."

With a rare display of petulance, she stamped her foot on the ground. "Don't imagine for one brief moment, my cousin will be distracted with worry at my absence. In all probability, she's setting up her new flirt at Devonshire House at this very minute."

"The thought had occurred to me," he answered with remarkable equanimity.

"Suddenly you don't appear to care!"

"Even so mediocre a wine can make a man see more clearly. She has used us both abominably, and I have it in mind to serve her out."

"Well, if you are thinking of punishing me, as I said . . ."

"Sit down, Miss. . . ." When she remained on her feet, he added with a touch of irritation in his voice, "Don't be so tiresome, girl. Do as you are told."

Amazed at her own submissiveness, she did sink down into the chair. She supposed the entire situation had taken on a dreamlike quality. She couldn't really be alone with the "most handsome man alive," moreover one who up until that day had scarcely been aware of her existence. A short time ago receiving this degree of attention, albeit hostile, from the "divine Carisbrooke"—Lady Hartnell's description—would have put her in heaven. Now his mood only alarmed her. She was alone and at his mercy. No one could even hazard a guess she was his unwilling guest except Kitty, and for very good reason she was not likely to say.

41

She gripped the arms of the chair until her knuckles grew white. Noting it, the marquess smiled and offered, "Take a glass of wine with me. It will do you good. Make you less fidgety."

"No. I thank you. You have consumed sufficient for both of us."

"You're not one of those prosy abstainers, are you?"

"Indeed not, but I do require a degree of companionship before I accept any kind of liquid refreshment."

"In that case, I won't trouble the landlord to provide you with lemonade."

Arabella started to get up again. "I believe I would like to go to my room. By the morrow I'm persuaded you will be better able to think in a more temperate manner and see the virtue of returning me to London."

"Balderdash!"

Startled, she sank down in the chair again, muttering, "This is indeed outrageous."

Ignoring her protest, he came across the room, bent down, and placed both hands on the arms of the chair, effectively imprisoning her there. His face was far too close to hers for true comfort, but there was no escape. Her heart beat an uneven tattoo as he asked, "What do you consider would be the worst calamity that could befall your cousin?"

Startled anew, she answered haltingly, "Sir Andrew losing his fortune, I suppose."

"Not likely. The worst we can hope for is for someone to come along and usurp her position in Society. Someone she least expects. A silly simpering debutante perhaps—or worse, her poor, overlooked drab of a cousin. A young lady of no importance, a chit to be ignored save when some inconsequential errand arises; someone worthy only of the most outmoded hand-me-down clothes . . ."

"Lord Carisbrooke, I protest! Insulting me in this vile manner will do nothing to alleviate your hurt feelings."

He looked triumphant as he straightened up. "Turning you into the talk of the Town certainly will."

She stared back at him in astonishment. "You're foxed!"

"Only a little bosky."

"Then you must be afflicted by the midsummer moon. That's it! Your attic's to let. You're fit for Bedlam."

"Even if I am, does it matter? Your life cannot be worse than it is at present."

With as much dignity as she could muster, Arabella replied, "My life is quite satisfactory, I thank you, my lord."

"I take leave to doubt it, but think how much more gratifying it would be if you were turned into a dasher, dressed in the high kick of fashion, sought after by those in the highest echelon of the ton."

"You *are* mad. How could you possibly achieve this amazing feat?"

"By marrying you, of course."

The statement was met by a momentary silence, and then she threw back her head and laughed uproariously as if she would never stop. When it seemed she couldn't stop, the marquess went up to her, pulled her out of the chair, and shook her roughly until the laughter finally drained out of her.

"You're afflicted by barrel-fever," she told him, still looking amused. "That is the only explanation for so bizarre a suggestion. I'm aware my cousin has always turned heads, but in your case I believe she has actually mangled your brain!"

He released her to go and pour out two glasses of wine. He handed one to Arabella, and this time she accepted and drank it down. A knock on the door heralded the arrival of the innkeeper.

"Anything more I can do for your worship?" he inquired in an unctuous tone.

Without taking his eyes off Arabella, Lord Carisbrooke snapped, "Leave us!" and the man swiftly went out again, closing the door behind him.

"Marriage to a madman can be no worse than what you are obliged to endure at present. You haven't considered the consequences of your cousin's attitude to you once she learns you have spent the night under the same roof as me."

"You are hateful," she cried.

"I promise you as a gentleman, I wouldn't tell, my dear, but I can't guarantee no one else would, and whatever else we say or think of your cousin, she is not slow-witted."

Arabella bit her lip as she contemplated, not for the first time, Kitty's reaction to the situation. Innocent or not, Arabella knew, this excursion would provoke Kitty's anger.

She walked slowly to the door, retaining as much dignity as she could. "At least I need not concern myself that my chances of making a good match have been compromised. Marriage was highly unlikely before this unfortunate journey began. I shall bid you good night, my lord, and trust that by the morrow you will be returned to both sobriety and good sense."

Chapter Six

*M*uch to Arabella's relief, the marquess did not attempt to stop her leaving the room, but the shabby bedchamber was the only place to go, and when she was at last alone with her thoughts, she was no less uneasy. Now a few insistent pangs of hunger added to her misery, but pride prevented her from going back to the parlor and partaking of some morsels of the unappetizing array of dishes. In retrospect, the food was somewhat appealing.

His anger and disappointment was no more than she had expected at the outset. A man as proud as he would not take Kitty's betrayal with equanimity, and although he appeared perfectly sober, she had seen him consuming copious amounts of inferior wine, so he was bound to be inebriated. A man so deep in his cups was never rational. Nonetheless, her cheeks grew warm as she recalled his proposal. She even smiled when she envisaged his embarrassment in the morning, unless, of course, he did not recall it at all, which was far more likely. That possibility afforded her a small crumb of comfort.

When she yawned and glanced longingly toward the bed, she didn't relish lying on it, let alone in it. Despite the sudden onset of fatigue, she couldn't imagine sleeping at all. Instead she seated herself in a chair and relived the extraordinary events of the evening over and over again in her mind until it all drifted away.

Suddenly she was wide awake, immediately aware the sounds of the inn had grown quiet. A deep darkness such as could only shroud the countryside had enveloped the hostelry, although there was some light in the room emanating from the embers of a fire and a tallow candle that still guttered in its tarnished holder.

All at once alert, Arabella jumped to her feet, knowing she had to escape this place. There was no certainty Lord Carisbrooke would apologize for his cavalier behavior and return her promptly to her cousin's mansion in Belgrave Square. He had indicated as much. Moreover, to rely upon the triumph of his good nature was to be far too trusting. He was not a man to cross, and it was not entirely inconceivable he'd been deadly serious in his proposal of marriage. Deranged—and that was how Arabella saw him—by the loss of Kitty, a crack-brained scheme to use her in an attempt to discompose her cousin could very well be a course he was seriously minded to follow. Arabella was equally resolved not to be used in that manner.

Panicked by her own sleepy thoughts, she hurried to the door and opened it a crack. There was no discernible noise from below, so she slipped on her cloak and picked up the candle. Shading it with her hand, she crept down the stairs, mercifully encountering no one in her flight. As she moved stealthily along the passageway, she could hear sounds coming from the public area of the inn and presumed some of the local inhabitants, as well as his lordship's servants, were still enjoying the landlord's hospitality.

The door was a stout one, and the hinges creaked as she slowly pulled it open; the noise seemed deafening. To make matters even worse, a stiff breeze was blowing and immediately whipped the door from her hand with unexpected fervor, flinging it back against the wall and extinguishing the candle.

The shock of the noise almost made her cry out. Instead she gasped, and before she could recover and make good her escape, the passageway flooded with light and a lazy voice inquired, "Going somewhere, my dear?"

Arabella whirled around on her heel to find the marquess standing in the parlor doorway, his arms folded across his chest. In his shirtsleeves, his neck cloth loosened, a thick lock of dark hair lying across his brow, he looked both handsome and devilish.

She saw no advantage in prevaricating, and admitted, "I was looking to escape."

"You'll come to more harm out there on your own than you ever will with me."

He held out his hand, and she stared at him implacably for some few moments before she relented and gave him the candlestick. After he'd relit the tallow candle with one from the parlor, she walked past him and preceded him up the stairs with her head held high. When she reached the bedchamber, he removed the large iron key from the keyhole.

"What are you going to do with that?" she demanded, suddenly fearful.

"Just ensuring you don't fall victim to a night-snap."

"I have nothing a thief might wish to steal."

His answer was to smile, and Arabella felt angry and helpless as he closed the door. She heard the key grating in the lock and then the sound of it being withdrawn.

"I won't be treated like a naughty child," she vowed, hurrying over to the window.

Mentally she assessed the possibility of reaching the ground safely, and knew it wouldn't be too difficult if she discarded Kitty's cloak. She was loath to do so but had no choice. It didn't matter that the casement creaked, for

47

Lord Carisbrooke wouldn't be able to hear it from the downstairs parlor, where she hoped he would be cosily settled with a full bottle of the inn's inferior wine. A clear night sky and a full moon were her accomplices, and very welcome they were too.

She opened the window as wide as it would go, startled momentarily by the cry of a nightjar. Then, hesitating no longer, she gathered up her skirts as far as she could, swinging first one leg and then the other over the window ledge. Holding on with one hand, she tested the ivy and found it to be well established. It would hold her weight easily. At that moment she envied gentlemen their breeches, for her skirts undoubtedly slowed her down. It seemed to take an inordinate time to reach the ground, but when she had done so, as she paused to brush off her hands and smooth down her skirts, she was unable to repress a chuckle.

The marquess was going to be so surprised in the morning when he unlocked the door and found her gone. By that time, with a little luck, she'd be well on her way to London—once she found the right road to take.

Before she had any opportunity to decide which direction she would follow from the inn, she was imprisoned by a pair of strong arms clasped about her body.

"Stop struggling," a familiar voice whispered close to her ear. "You're in luck—it's only me."

Arabella sagged in the marquess's arms, tears of frustration stinging her eyes. "I thought you might try something of this nature," he told her, "although where you hope to go or what I have done to induce you to resort to such measures, I cannot conceive."

"Perhaps you do this all the time, but I can assure you, my lord, being imprisoned against my will is not a normal circumstance to me!"

"Then, this is bound to add considerable spice to your

existence." When she gasped with annoyance, his grip loosened a little, although he didn't let her go. "How old are you?"

"Three and twenty."

"A little old for such hoydenish jinks."

"The situation is extraordinary."

"Climbing from an upstairs window and showing your—admittedly shapely—ankles, is not exactly the behavior of a lady."

Although being held against the marquess's powerful body was not precisely unpleasant, Arabella belatedly twisted out of his grasp, turning to face him and retorting in a harsh whisper, "Abduction is not the conduct of a gentleman."

"I offered to put matters to rights in the most drastic way," he replied as he took her arm and led her back into the inn. "No one could possibly undertake to do more."

"You don't expect me to marry a gentleman who cannot even remember my name."

He chuckled as he led her upstairs, and she had the uncomfortable feeling he had begun to enjoy the situation. "Arabella," he murmured, and her heart gave a little lurch at the sound of her name on his lips.

"Say it again in the morning."

"If I do, will you agree to marry me?"

She didn't answer. She merely watched as he unlocked the door, then rushed into the bedchamber. She was not prepared for him to follow her, locking the door behind them this time and placing the key in his waistcoat pocket.

"What *are* you doing?" she demanded, moving quickly to the far side of the room.

"Making certain we both have a night's sleep with no further distraction."

"I'm beginning to feel hungry," she admitted.

"All the food—if, indeed, it can be described as that—has been cleared away," he replied as he glanced around him with evident distaste. "You should have eaten when it was offered to you."

"I wasn't hungry then."

He gave her his attention once more. "I do hope you're not going to spend what remains of the night bleating."

"If I do, I'll consider myself entitled. I believe I have been treated most unfairly."

"Not as unfairly as I," he countered. "Now, do be quiet."

From her guarded position at the far side of the room, she watched mutinously as he seated himself in the chair she had previously occupied, thrusting his long legs out in front of him. He rested his head on the chair back and closed his eyes. Arabella continued to observe him for some few minutes, sure he was only feigning sleep. At last, she realized she couldn't remain standing for what was left of the night and sank down uneasily on the edge of the bed. Finally, sheer exhaustion forced her to lay down and eventually fall into a dreamless sleep.

There were few customers in the snug of the Jolly Hangman. Lord Carisbrooke's servants were huddled in one corner drinking the inferior ale and discussing quietly their master's odd behavior. None of them, it was agreed, had ever observed his lordship disport himself in so eccentric a manner.

Barstow, the innkeeper, eyed them keenly until the outer door opened and a tall gentleman in shabby clothes and battered beaver hat strolled in.

One shaggy eyebrow shot up at the sight of the strangers. "What's to do?" he asked quietly, cocking his head in their direction, when he reached the bar.

"We've got quality staying," the landlord answered proudly.

"Quality, eh? My, my," the newcomer murmured, "this place'll soon be too toplofty for the likes of me."

"You know Tom Barstow'll always look after his friends. What can I get yer?"

"A tankard of heavy-wet, I thankee."

After serving the muddy liquid, the landlord leaned forward in a conspiratorial manner. "It's a real rum do. Says he's traveling with his sister, but to me they 'ave the look of a pair of runaways."

The other man's eyes narrowed. "Do they, now?"

"Aye. Heard them go upstairs together a time ago, and there they are still—as snug as two bugs in a rug."

"Sounds like havey-cavey business to me. No one who considers themselves quality would choose to stay here unless it was a queer start."

"Now, just a minute, Mattie! There's no need to do it too brown!"

The other man ignored the landlord's outrage and mused, "Perchance, Tom, there's something in this for me and thee."

"Like what?" the innkeeper asked, immediately forgetting the insult.

"Don't rightly know as yet, but if the chit's a runaway, guaranteed there's an anxious papa waiting for news of her." As Tom Barstow nodded sagely, his friend asked, "What's this gentry cove's name?"

"Don't know. He didn't say."

"That's suspicious for a start. Gentry coves like their names to be recognized wherever they go. What about the gentry mort?"

"Don't know hers neither, but Bertha tells me she's all of a bobble."

The newcomer glanced back to where Windle and the

footmen were drinking and talking quietly among themselves. "Let's have some more ale for those fellows, Tommy. See if we can't loosen their tongues."

The innkeeper appeared momentarily pleased at the suggestion, and then he frowned. "Now, who is going to pay their shot, Mattie?"

The other man laughed softly. "You're going to stand the shock, my friend." At the sight of the landlord's startled expression, he explained with a sly wink, "You've got to speculate to accumulate!"

"What a splendid hurricane that was," Sir Andrew Polstead observed as his carriage rattled into the drive of his London house.

"It's always a pink night at the Devonshires," his wife replied, startled out of her thoughts.

Behind her carefully cultivated ease, she was in a fidge to hear from Arabella's lips what had transpired with Lord Carisbrooke. This was the first time any of her fancies had taken the drastic step of suggesting elopement, and she was both fearful and excited for the outcome. Naturally, while she hoped news of the marquess's desire to run off with her to Paris would become public knowledge, she was aware no one could possibly blame her for his outrageous conduct. She had done nothing to encourage him in his mad pursuit of her, save what was permissible in a married lady. Everyone knew she was devoted to Sir Andrew and their child. Still, in the absence of Lord Carisbrooke, young Lord Loudon had been most attentive that evening, she mused, smiling faintly in a darkness punctuated only by the flares held aloft by the running footmen.

"And you, my dear," Sir Andrew went on, "were the most beautiful woman present this evening. I was only relieved Carisbrooke wasn't there, acting like a barnacle.

It gave others the undoubted pleasure of enjoying your company."

Lady Polstead's ready smile faded, and when the carriage came to a halt at the front door, her husband climbed down and offered her his hand.

While the night porter took their cloaks, Sir Andrew informed his wife, "I believe I shall take a glass of brandy before I retire."

Relieved, Kitty fled up the stairs and immediately encountered a maidservant who was walking along the corridor carrying a warming pan. "Have you seen my cousin, Miss Trentham, this evening?"

"No, my lady, I haven't so much as clapped eyes on her."

"Don't stand there like a gapeseed! Find her! She's often ensconced with Miss Polstead—or with her nose in a book. Instruct all the other servants to find her, and send her to me on the bustle! Do you understand?"

The frightened maidservant curtsied and scurried away to do her mistress's bidding while Lady Polstead burst into her bedchamber and threw her reticule and fan down on the bed, startling her abigail, who had been snoozing by the fire.

"Unhook me, Temple." When the elderly maidservant struggled to her feet, her mistress raged, "I looked positively fat tonight, Temple. Do you know that?"

"Your ladyship looked as lovely as she always does."

"Allow me to be the judge of that! You didn't lace me tight enough, even though I always entreat you to do so. Oh, do be quick! You're getting so slow I'll be obliged to replace you soon."

"You know you won't do that, my lady. Temple's too useful to your ladyship. No one cares for you as well as I do."

"Because of your indisposition, I was obliged to send my cousin on a declicate errand."

"I'm sorry about that, ma'am."

"Now she is nowhere to be found. I don't suppose *you* have seen her."

Temple unhooked her mistress's gown and began to unlace her stays. "No, my lady, I haven't seen hide or hair of the young lady all day."

"Oh, it really is too bad! Just when it's imperative I speak to her, she plays least in sight! I shouldn't be surprised if she's done this on purpose to vex me, knowing I'd be in a fidge to learn what went on. She's usually with Molly, or in the servant's hall, or with her nose in a book. I can always find that tiresome, predictable creature—except *now*. Oh, it really is too bad. She's such an ingrate."

"She can't have gone far, my lady, for it's understood Miss Trentham doesn't know anyone else in town."

"I hope not! She's wearing my sable-trimmed cloak."

Just as she slipped her arms into her peignoir, the door opened and Kitty Polstead turned on her heel, a frown marring her fabled beauty. "At last and not before time."

However, it was Sir Andrew who entered the room and not Arabella. "It gladdens my heart to find you anxious for your husband's attention after so many years of marriage. What a compliment that is. Good night, Temple," Andrew said pointedly.

Lady Polstead bit back an angry retort and cast her husband a smile while seething inwardly at her cousin's continued absence. Now she wouldn't be able to speak to her until the morning, ensuring a sleepless night and, like as not, dark circles under her eyes. Her ladyship silently vowed that Arabella would be very sorry indeed.

Chapter Seven

Arabella awoke with a start, momentarily puzzled by her strange surroundings. Then, as an uncharacteristically disheveled marquess loomed over her, she shrank back into the lumpy pillow.

"Come along," he ordered and then, when she shrank back even more, he added irritably, "Oh, for heaven's sake, there's no need for you to behave like an old maid. It's time to leave. I've had my fill of this flea-pit."

"It's no one's fault but your own that we're here," she accused as she struggled to sit up.

Lord Carisbrooke moved to the door, drawing out the key and inserting it into the lock. Arabella continued to watch him with scarce concealed resentment as he struggled with the lock.

"What the devil?" he gasped. She found it difficult to suppress a giggle at witnessing the great Corinthian experiencing so much difficulty opening an ill-fitting door. "The key turns easily, but the door is still securely locked."

He rattled the knob and then banged on the door with the flat of his hand. Finally he put one broad shoulder to the door, which still remained firmly shut.

Arabella's amusement faded at last. "What . . . what appears to be the problem?"

He ran one hand through his dark curls before he declared, "I suspect the rascally landlord has us locked in."

"Why would he wish to do that?"

"Probably because he can envisage some gain by keeping us here." He began to hammer on the door again, shouting, "Come up here, you cowardly weasel. Open the door, and you'll see what a basting you'll get!"

"Don't you think that is likely to frighten him away rather than encourage him to open the door?" Arabella asked timidly.

"What is your suggestion?" the angry marquess inquired, and she was forced to look away from his dark stare, which was even more disturbing when he was in the grip of such wrath.

"I have no notion," she confessed.

"Then, be pleased to remain silent until you do have something useful to suggest."

"I don't see why I should. I am held here against my will."

"Now we both are!" At that moment footsteps could be heard coming up the stairs, and the marquess called out, "Open the door landlord, and we'll be gone with no more ado."

"You'll 'ave to wait a while, till the young lady's father arrives."

"What are you gabbling on about, you idiot?"

The landlord chuckled at the other side of the door. "Didn't think you fooled Tom Barstow with the tale about your *sister*, did you? Tom Barstow's fly to the time of day all right. I knows a runaway couple when I sees one. Now, don't you make any more fuss, because there's no one to hear you."

"Hell and damnation!" Lord Carisbrooke cried to the receding footsteps of the innkeeper. "Come back

56

here, you blockhead," he roared after the footsteps had died away.

"You really handled that situation with great diplomacy, my lord," Arabella told him.

"I didn't hear you suggesting anything better." Then he added, "Come along, we're not going to be held to ransom by some rascally chaw-bacon. We'll have to leave by the window."

While he strode across the room and opened the casement, she stared at him in horror. "My father is dead. Who is he sending to fetch?"

"Heaven only knows what is going on in that pottage he calls a brain, but one thing I do know, we are not waiting around to find out. Come along, Miss . . . don't hang in the hedge there. You go first."

Arabella shrank back. "No, I shan't."

"Don't be ridiculous," he roared, causing her to flinch away even further. "Do you want to stay in this den of iniquity?"

"I have no wish to climb down a sheer wall."

"You had no compunction last evening."

"That was different."

A frown beetled his dark brows. "Very well," he said resignedly, "I shall climb down carrying you over my shoulder. I'll try very hard not to drop you, but there's no certainty that I won't."

When he approached her with a purposeful air, she shrank back even more. "There is no need. I'll go."

"First," he added.

As she looped up her skirts, he didn't trouble to glance away, but she reckoned his glimpse of her ankles was not her most pressing concern just then. He helped her over the ledge, and she discovered it was easier than the last time, because of the daylight and her knowledge that the ivy was strong enough to hold her weight. Once she reached the ground, the marquess climbed out of the window, and with an agility she could only admire, he joined her within a few seconds.

Arabella grinned when she looked at him, his neck cloth awry, his shirt grubby, and his hair rumpled. "I've never seen you look so disheveled before."

"I don't suppose anyone has since I was in short coats."

"I daresay your valet is waiting for you in Paris."

"You are entirely mistaken about that, Miss Knownothing. By the by, have you seen yourself this morning?"

Even as he spoke, she caught sight of her own reflection in a windowpane and gasped. Her shabby dress had the added disadvantage of being crumpled and soiled. Her hair had come loose from its pins and drifted in untidy wisps across her face, and she was sure she detected streaks of dirt on her cheeks.

"Come on," he urged, taking hold of her hand. "Let's find the stables. I've no notion how many blackguards infest this place, but the sooner we leave the better I will like it."

He pulled her after him across the cobbles, Arabella glancing behind every few seconds only to receive an impatient tug on her hand from the marquess. They entered the stables by a side door, certain they hadn't been observed from the inn.

It was a great relief to both of them to find the carriage in place and the horses munching contentedly at their hay. However, that feeling quickly evaporated on hearing a deafening chorus of snores coming from one corner of the stable.

After exchanging curious glances with the marquess, Arabella followed him to where the noise was originating.

"My stars!" he cried when he saw the insensible figures of his servants.

He prodded Windle with the toe of his boot, and the driver briefly rallied only to sink back into the hay with a resounding snore. The marquess repeated the exercise with the other men before becoming more vociferous.

"Come along, you lazy, jug-bitten scaff and raff! Rouse yourselves!" Then he looked at Arabella with a despairing glance that actually made him appear human. "It's no use. These lobcocks aren't going to drive us anywhere."

"They're all as drunk as wheelbarrows!"

"It must have been quite a carouse last night." He bent down and roughly manhandled each of his servants in turn until he got them to their feet and then pushed them somewhat brutally into the carriage, slamming the door behind them before he sank back against the coachwork to catch his breath.

"Now, what are we to do?" Arabella asked in a hushed whisper.

At the sound of her voice, he straightened up again, "You are going to help me couple the horses." Biting back a word of protest, she followed him to where the animals were standing. "Come along," he urged. "We need to be as quick as we can. Time is of the essence, girl."

"My name is Miss Trentham," she reminded him with as much dignity as she could muster.

"Yes, yes, I remember, but this isn't the time to stand on points. Just take one of the horses and slip the harness over his head and fasten it to the shafts . . . no, no, not that one, child. He's a leader. He needs to be at the front."

Irritably she retorted, "How am I to know a leader from a wheeler? Or a thruster for that matter? I've never been obliged to put to before."

"Then, observe me carefully, and regard it as a

valuable lesson that could stand you in good stead in the future."

"Yes, I might well be consigned to the stables after this little excursion."

The horse evidently sensed her nervousness and skittered, causing the buckles to slip from her fingers, while her companion worked swiftly and accurately at the other side of the carriage. Eventually he came to her side of the shafts and took charge.

"We'll still be here at dinnertime if you don't get on the bustle, Miss Trentham."

Vaguely aware he actually called her by her name, Arabella retorted, "I doubt if my cousin would have been of any greater use to you in these circumstances, so don't be so scathing of me!"

To her surprise, he laughed. "Lady Polstead requires a half dozen servants just to attend her down the stairs. I don't suppose even you are quite as demanding as that."

"I don't require servants to help me in anything I do, my lord. I am perfectly accustomed to doing everything for myself."

"Small wonder your cousin finds you so irritating if you always open your budget in this way."

Arabella had no opportunity to express her dismay at his words, for he had fastened the last strap and began to usher her around to the side of the carriage. "Get inside, and we can be off with no further delay."

She resisted his hold on her, declaring, "I have no intention of traveling an inch in close company with your bosky servants."

An expression of irritation crossed his face. "I do believe you've come along in order to vex me."

"If you recall correctly, my lord, I didn't choose to come along at all. I was brought here against my will."

"That was my second mistake."

"What was your first?" she had to ask.

Before she had a chance to realize what he intended to do, he seized her by the waist and lifted her onto the box. In the brief moment he held her, she sensed the strength in him. It was no effort at all for him to place her firmly on the box.

"Becoming entangled with your cousin was my first mistake," he answered at last.

He went to pull open first one stable door and then the other as quickly and as quietly as he could before turning to the carriage and climbing up next to Arabella. He took up the ribbons and after whispering, "Hold hard there, Miss Trentham," he called, "Gee hup!" and the team lurched forward, pulling the carriage out of the building, through the yard, and past the hostelry itself.

The commotion brought the landlord and his wife running out of the inn, their hands raised in horror. The marquess saluted them smartly with the tip of his whip as the carriage thundered past and out into the open road without a sign of pursuit.

Arabella glanced back to see the couple flapping their arms impotently up and down, like automatons she had once seen at a fair, their figures growing ever more distant. Ignoring the sounds of distress emanating from within the carriage, she turned her attention to the marquess.

"We've escaped!" she gasped. "I really didn't think we could do it."

He glanced at her and grinned, while not allowing the horses to slow in the slightest. His gray eyes were less cold than she had noted before, his ruffled hair rendered him less formidable, and at that moment she felt there was a rare camaraderie between them that bestowed on her the oddest sensation of warmth.

"You surely didn't believe I'd allow a pair of ignorant rustics to hold us to ransom, did you?"

The feeling of liberation was heady, and Arabella began to laugh as the wind tore at her already disordered curls. He laughed too. They had traveled several miles down the road before she recalled she was still far from free and she had no notion where he was taking her.

"What do you mean she hasn't been seen since before dinner!" Lady Polstead raged at her house steward. "*I* saw her before dinner. Someone must have seen her since."

"I have made inquiries, my lady, and I assure you Miss Trentham is not in the house. It was reported to Mrs. Dingle that the young lady does not appear to have slept in her bed."

"Impossible," her ladyship cried, and then, as she turned on her heel in an attempt to control her fear and apprehension, she caught sight of her daughter crouching down by the landing, peering through the balustrade. "Molly, come down here this minute."

The girl straightened slowly and with much reluctance came down the stairs to face her mother. Molly as much as anyone knew when it was best to keep out of Lady Polstead's path, and this was definitely one of those occasions.

"Now, Molly," Lady Polstead began with scarce concealed impatience, "I am trying to locate our cousin. I'm persuaded you must know where she is."

"No, Mama, I don't."

"Don't lie to me, Molly!"

"I wouldn't do that, Mama. Miss Byford says it's wicked to lie. I haven't seen Arabella since teatime yesterday. She promised to have dinner with me in the nursery, but she didn't come. Mama, has something terrible happened to Bella?"

"Not yet," her mother murmured under her breath, and then, aware it would be politic not to make too much of an issue out of her cousin's disappearance, she gave her daughter a conciliatory smile. "No, indeed, my love. You mustn't trouble your head, and I know I am a widgeon to concern myself in this manner. If only your cousin wasn't so dear to me. . . . I am persuaded there is a very good reason for her absence."

Sometime later, accompanied by her trusted abigail, her ladyship walked the short distance to Carisbrooke House in Grosvenor Square. The house steward appeared startled to see her when he came to the door.

"Be so good as to inform Lord Carisbrooke that Lady Polstead is here," she informed him in the imperious manner she employed toward servants.

"I regret to inform you, my lady, his lordship is no longer in town. As you might have noticed when you arrived, the knocker has been removed from the door, indicating he has no intention of returning in the near future."

Struggling to retain her calm, she asked, "Where, pray, has his lordship gone?"

"I am given to understand he has gone to the Continent, my lady, and is not expected to return for some months." He didn't add that the entire household of servants assumed their master had gone with the very person standing before him.

"Do you think Miss Trentham might have met with an accident, or foul play, on her way back to the house?" Temple asked when they were outside.

Lady Polstead began to walk purposefully away from her lover's house, where she had enjoyed so many blissful hours. "If that is so, we may never know what happened to her."

"You could make inquiries, my lady."

Irritably she replied, "I cannot be expected to trawl 'round the charnel houses of London in search of her body. For heaven's sake, Temple, you didn't mean to suggest I would want to visit hospitals and the like in search of my cousin, who it appears was unable to get herself to the corner of Park Street and back again without encountering some mishap."

"You could send one of the servants."

"Indeed not. I could not expect one of my servants to embark upon an errand I would not be willing to undertake myself. I cannot pursue this matter any further, for fear of inviting too many awkward questions. I've a mind to visit Swan and Edgar to buy some gewgaws. That never fails to raise my spirits. Let's return to the house and order my carriage to be brought 'round."

By the time she returned home with her numerous packages, Lady Polstead had to acknowledge her spirits were just as low as before, and the sight of her husband in the hall did nothing to raise them.

"Kitty, what's to do? The house is in an uproar. Everyone is searching for Arabella."

Lady Polstead carefully removed her poke-brimmed bonnet, which left not a hair out of place. "It is all a nothing, dearest, and I would not have you trouble your head. It's a mistake."

With Lord Carisbrooke gone to the Continent, the immediate fear of embarrassment had been removed. By the time he returned, their liaison would be long-forgotten. As for Arabella, it seemed clear now she had met with foul play. The streets of London were growing ever more perilous, particularly for a female alone. It was likely she'd become just another victim, unclaimed and buried in a pauper's grave.

Lady Polstead drew a sigh as her husband asked, "Do you know where she has gone?"

"Indeed." Her expression was artless as she went on to explain, "It has transpired that late yesterday she received a note from an elderly aunt who resides in Bath. The poor dear is gravely ill, and being such a compassionate creature, Arabella felt obliged to go there to give her whatever comfort she could. The confusion arose when the note she left informing me of her errand was briefly overlooked. I have no notion when she'll be able to return."

Sir Andrew frowned. "An aunt you say? In Bath? I had no notion either of you had other relatives alive."

"The woman is a great-aunt on her father's side. No relation of mine, I might add."

To her relief, Sir Andrew appeared to accept the explanation, and after he had returned to his study, she picked up a posy that had arrived in her absence. Lord Loudon's card was dangling from it, and she buried her face in the fragrant blooms, determined not to give either Lord Carisbrooke or Arabella another moment's thought.

Chapter Eight

$\mathcal{A}$uden End, seat of the Marquess of Carisbrooke, was reputed to be one of the loveliest houses in England, so when the carriage swept through a pair of tall gates and the house came into view a few minutes later, Arabella was surprised at what she saw. The rambling mansion was a veritable hotchpotch of styles, extensive gothic turrets interspersed with tower rooms, all topped off by a great cupola.

"This really is going too far," she protested.

"Yes, I know, but I couldn't think what else to do with you," he answered frankly.

After drawing up outside the house he leaped down from the box and came around to her side of the carriage. Once again, before she had any chance to prepare herself, he was lifting her down. Arabella had the impression of being suspended momentarily in midair as he gazed into her eyes. By the time he'd deposited her at the bottom of the broad flight of steps that led up to the front door, she felt somewhat breathless.

"I am sorely disappointed, my lord," she told him a moment later.

He glanced up at the house before answering, "It isn't the most pleasing of edifices, I confess."

"I was not alluding to the house," she answered through her teeth. "I did consider after this morning's adventures, you would have the goodness to return me to London."

"Your cousin will have noticed you're missing by now."

"Does that matter?" she snapped. "It isn't too late to send me back. I'm sure you must have a spare carriage and team at your disposal."

"You can't want to travel alone."

"I've done it before."

"How would you explain your absence?"

"I'd think of something."

"It'll wait. You can't go anywhere looking as you do, and neither can I."

"I don't believe it wise to go inside with you, my lord."

A look of irritation crossed his handsome features. "You should have thought of the consequences before you agreed to undertake your cousin's dirty work."

"Do you truly believe I had any choice?"

"You have even less now," was his maddening reply before he started up the steps.

Arabella hesitated briefly. Feeling helpless while those around her ordered her life was not a new experience, but in these particular circumstances, it was especially vexing. Those ladies who adored him from afar had no notion how provoking he could be.

"How long do you intend to keep me here?" she asked breathlessly when she caught up with him.

"Until I can think of a solution. I can scarce drive up to Polstead House with you beside me on the box. That really would send the tattle baskets on a gabster's marathon."

"My rep is of no importance to anyone but me."

He grinned roguishly. "On the other hand, my rep is of interest to everyone and won't be enhanced one jot by being linked with yours."

Arabella stiffened with outrage. "Lord Carisbrooke, I declare you to be quite the most odious gentleman I have ever encountered in my entire life!"

He stared at her consideringly for much too long a time for Arabella's comfort before he replied, "That is an unusual opinion in any young lady of my acquaintance, but you might well have overlooked the fact that even I cannot expect to spend the night with a chit of a girl who is as well connected as you, and escape the consequences."

"I promise you, I have absolutely no import whatsoever in the Polstead household and in Society in general. No one will pursue you with a blunderbuss."

"My honor has also been compromised, ma'am, and this situation needs a good deal of consideration before a solution is like to present itself."

Her lips twisted into a smile of derision. "You're so stiff-rumped," she told him in exasperation. "It's outside of enough."

"You're not the first to say so. Ah, good day to you Postlethwaite," he greeted the house steward with infuriating good humor. "Both my guest and myself need bathwater, followed by a cold collation as soon as you please."

As the marquess strode toward the stairs, he added, "Mrs. Postlethwaite will attend you, Miss Trentham. We'll meet again later."

"Not if I can possibly help it," she muttered beneath her breath.

"This way, madam," the housekeeper indicated with scarce concealed disapproval.

Arabella didn't doubt the blame for all this would fall squarely on her slender shoulders. She had every expectation that his lordship would escape all censure. Worse still, Kitty would vilify her for what had happened. It was an impossible situation, and one from which she could envisage no escape.

Sometime later Arabella came hesitantly down the stairs. She had bathed, and the housekeeper had done her best to clean her gown and repair several small tears in the material. Glancing in the cheval mirror, it occurred to Arabella that she looked like a tatterdemalion and when she eventually returned to Polstead House she'd better have a very good story ready.

The bath had certainly been welcome, as had the excellent repast brought to her on a tray. Now she felt invigorated and relieved she encountered no one in the hall. She let herself out of the main door, then hurried down the steps. In the distance the sun was glinting off a lake, and in front of the house a large fountain was set in the middle of an ornate parterre garden.

She couldn't allow herself time to pause and admire her surroundings, for she was sure she had only a short time to effect her escape. Although convinced Lord Carisbrooke had been the worse for drink the previous evening and certain he had forgotten his proposal of marriage, she couldn't be absolutely positive he wasn't intending to use her in some other manner to punish Kitty.

Being entirely unfamiliar with the estate, she had no option but to follow a path that led around the back of the house, passing a walled garden and then a maze. When a wood loomed up before her, Arabella accepted there was no way of escape in that direction. Disappointed but not deterred, she returned the way she had come. Again, when she reached the house, she was relieved not to encounter anyone except a couple of gardeners who, not knowing whether she was quality or not, merely nodded respectfully in her direction.

This time her choice of direction paid off when she spied the large stable block ahead of her. There was no sign of the carriage, and when she spotted a lone stable lad, she said in as imperious a manner as she could contrive, "Saddle me a horse, will you? And be quick about it."

"I'm afraid I can't do that, ma'am, not without his lordship's say-so."

"That's outrageous!" she protested, her self-confidence immediately fading. "I insist you do as I ask."

"It's orders, ma'am."

"To the devil with you!" she cried.

Tears of frustration were stinging her eyes as she turned on her heel, only to walk slap into the marquess, who was now looking more as she was accustomed to seeing him. He was wearing a forest green riding coat, clean breeches, and a perfectly folded neck cloth. That he looked as handsome as ever did nothing to ease her frustration.

"Whoa there!" he said, catching hold of her by the arms. "What's the hurry?"

His eyes were filled with amusement, and as she detached herself from his grip with studied deliberation, she answered, "I believe you know perfectly well."

"You'll only get into deeper trouble out there on your own."

"So you keep saying, but I cannot envisage anything worse than this."

There was a twinkle in his eye when he answered, "Can't you? Just wait until you see your cousin again, and you will certainly find out."

Suddenly she cast him a curious look. "I'm bound to say you no longer appear devastated by her treachery."

"I'm angry with myself. I have rarely been so foolish."

"A folly compounded by abducting me."

"Yes," he agreed, "but I'm not a cad, and I hope to put the matter to rights with no further delay. We can discuss it later. Will you join me for dinner?"

An invitation for dinner from the divine marquess was something almost every female must dream about, she thought. A word from his lips was sufficient to turn a mundane function into a brilliant occasion for even the most sophisticated young ladies. Two nights ago he hadn't even known she existed, and now she commanded his complete attention. Naturally, the drawback was that once she was back in London, she couldn't boast of it to anyone.

"Miss Trentham?"

His voice broke into her thoughts, and unable to trust herself to reply, she merely brushed past him and rushed back into the house.

Chapter Nine

*W*hen Arabella was ushered into the dimly lit dining room later that afternoon, she felt the situation strangely unreal. Mrs. Postlethwaite had found her a gown to wear, one of red velvet with swansdown trimming, adorning a neckline somewhat lower than she was accustomed to sporting. The housekeeper apologized profusely for the outmoded style of the garment, but truthfully it was far more beautiful than any Arabella had worn before.

Lord Carisbrooke was standing by the fireplace, a glass in his hand, and he looked so handsome in evening dress, her heart almost stopped before racing wildly, as if to make up for the omission.

He observed her in silence for a few moments that seemed endless before saying to her great surprise, "How fetching you look." Her cheeks flushed almost to the color of the gown when he added to her chagrin, "I had no notion you could look so fine."

"Thank you, my lord," she answered, averting her eyes and making no attempt to hide her sarcasm.

When they were seated, he at the head of the long mahogany table, she at his right hand, the servants brought in the various dishes. "We'll enjoy a very different meal to the one we were obliged to accept last night," he murmured.

"I didn't sample last night's. This place isn't at all

what I expected," she told him a moment later. "Everyone talks of Auden End as being so lovely. . . ."

He looked up momentarily. As his eyes narrowed in the candlelight, she noticed the length of his lashes. "This isn't Auden End." Arabella started, and he added, "I wouldn't be crack-brained enough to bring you to my own house."

"What is this place, then? Your hunting box?"

The food did indeed look appetizing, and the marquess watched in amusement as she heaped her plate with great gusto. "It's my cousin's place. No one will find us until I choose to let them."

She was again discomforted at the tacit reminder that she was here unwillingly and subject to his every whim. Up until the last four and twenty hours, she had known him only as every debutante's desire—the most handsome man alive. He might also be the most evil, for all she knew of him.

It was the marquess who chattered to ease any awkward moment during the meal. "Tell me about yourself, Miss Trentham," he asked at last.

"There isn't a great deal to divulge, I'm afraid."

"How exactly are you related to Kitty Polstead?"

She noted his voice grew hard as he spoke, and she regretted the introduction of Kitty's name. "She's my cousin. My only relative apart from Molly, of course. Our mothers were sisters. I had a brother, but he fell at Trafalgar."

"I'm sorry to hear that," he murmured as he raised his glass.

Arabella toyed with the stem of her own glass. "We weren't close, although I miss him now. He was a good deal older than I."

"Why is it Lady Polstead is so full of juice, and you are on the rocks?"

"My father was a tutor. He earned very little, and the only homes we had were those provided by his employers. When he died, I was left with nothing in the way of material goods. Kitty's father was a country parson in similarly straightened circumstances. However, she was taken up by one of her father's wealthy parishioners, Mrs. Pendle-Stroud, and it was at one of her house parties that she was introduced to Sir Andrew. I understand he fell head over tip in love with her at first sight." Although he appeared intent upon his food, she noted that the marquess's jaw seemed to clench at her last revelation. "After Papa died, Kitty was good enough to take me in."

"But not good enough to provide you with a modest portion and a Season of your own."

Arabella stiffened with indignation. "I did not expect one, my lord," she answered, coming to her cousin's defense. "Her generosity was sufficient."

She eyed the mouthwatering array of puddings, selecting a portion of particularly inviting syllabub. While she finished it off with relish, she said without daring to look at him, "Kitty's a terrible flirt, but she is devoted to Sir Andrew."

"So I have discovered." His voice was dripping with irony.

"You are greatly mistaken if you regard Kitty as illused by Sir Andrew. I assure you, she is not." When he made no reply, she ventured, "You mustn't allow this . . . unfortunate incident to color your life."

"I won't." He'd become amused again. A moment later he leaned forward, asking, "Would you care for anything more?"

She sat back in the chair and cast him an abashed smile. "I really have had enough."

"The fruit at Abbey Dulcis is excellent. My cousin cultivates all species with great success. Here . . ." He plucked a succulent peach from a silver-gilt epergne, and handed it to her.

As he did so, her gaze met his, and she was shocked by the passion she saw lurking in their depths, enhanced by the flickering candlelight. When she accepted the peach, their hands touched, and Arabella felt a charge pass through her that induced her to withdraw abruptly. The peach slipped from her grasp, rolling onto the floor, its progress ignored as she was unable to drag her gaze away from his. It was retrieved by a footman who sprang forward before he handed her another fruit from the table.

"I think it time for me to withdraw and leave you to your port, my lord," she told him hurriedly, her voice uneven.

"I'll forgo that particular pleasure this evening. We have something to discuss. Matters of great import that cannot be delayed any longer, don't you agree?"

They waited in silence for the servants to withdraw, which seemed to take a very long time, during which Arabella experienced a return of her apprehension. She had spent the previous night locked in a bedchamber with him, but she had never felt more self-conscious than she did now.

Eventually when the servants had withdrawn, he pushed back his chair and went to the fireplace, staring into its leaping flames.

After a few moments Arabella cleared her throat, and ventured, "If you provide me with transport, I could just return to London on my own."

"Just!" he scoffed without looking up. "What in tarnation would you say when you arrived?"

"I have been thinking about that all afternoon. There was a story in the *Morning Post* a few months ago. You might recall it yourself. A young lady went out to the circulating library to borrow a book, and didn't return home for five whole days. She had no notion where she had been."

"You weren't going to the library—you were meeting me. Lady Polstead knows it full well and wouldn't believe that Banbury tale for a moment. She'd have the true story out of you in a trice."

"Even if she did, she wouldn't be able to do anything about it without implicating herself."

"Perhaps not, but she would certainly make your life miserable for the foreseeable future, and you must have a remarkable tolerance for suffering if you are so eager to return to that." Arabella eyed him resentfully as he raised his head and asked, "Have you given any further thought to the proposal I put to you last night?"

Unconsciously she toyed with the peach, which she'd made no attempt to eat. "Naturally not. I didn't take it seriously. You were distressed, not to say foxed into the bargain."

He turned his back on the fire and straightened up, clasping his hands behind his back. "I am not foxed now, nor am I in the least distressed. I am deadly serious."

She shrank back into the chair with alarm, and he mocked, "Is your life with Lady Polstead so wonderful you are loath to leave it? Recall she is as like as anything to turn you out when you return."

"She wouldn't!"

"Can you be so sure?" When she averted her eyes from his, he went on in a dispassionate tone that cut her more surely than his sarcasm. "Miss Trentham, I am offering you my name, a chance to make an advantageous match instead of living as a poor relation at the beck and call of a peevish woman for the rest of your life. You'd possess a prominent position in Society."

76

She looked away from him in distress. "I'm not sure I want one."

"Nonsense! Every female I have ever encountered wants what I am offering you."

"Why would you wish to marry me?" she asked, totally bewildered.

"For the reason I have already declared. I have a mind to serve her out, and I can think of nothing more likely to do so than elevating you. Lady Polstead will tolerate no rivals, much less her drab of a cousin."

"How flattering to be used so," she answered, and there was no disguising her bitterness.

"We are not talking about a love match, just a business proposition that will be beneficial to you."

Arabella laughed harshly. "I'd have no notion how to go about being your wife. I couldn't possibly be a rival to Kitty. Her position in Society is unassailable. She has worked long and hard to achieve it."

"Fashion and fancy in the beau monde is very capricious. Novelty is all, and you are nothing if not unusual. You would soon learn all that is necessary. I would make certain of that," he added darkly. "When it is over, you'll still bear my name, possess a fine house and carriage with servants of your own. You would have everything you could possibly desire. Wouldn't that be far better than what you have to look forward to at the present?"

She stared sightlessly into the flames of the fire, tears blurring her vision. Of course she wanted to become Lady Carisbrooke. She could think of nothing more sublime than to be the wife of the most eligible man in London, but not for those reasons. Kitty had used her—Arabella understood that. Lady Polstead had a reason to expect some return for her charity, but she didn't want to be exploited by this man.

"What you ask of me is impossible. In the first instance

I am not up to such a task, and secondly, even if I were, I couldn't repay my cousin's charity by such disloyalty. Whatever she has done to you, she gave me a home when there was no other."

"No, she didn't," he told her, and his steely gaze never left her. "It was Sir Andrew who insisted they take you in. Lady Polstead told me so herself. She would have consigned you to the workhouse without a passing thought."

Arabella jumped to her feet with such agitation, the lyre-backed Sheraton chair crashed to the floor. "You lie!" she cried and then, unable to conceal her heartbreak, she turned on her heel and ran toward the door.

The marquess dashed after her, and just as she opened the door, he slammed it shut, keeping the flat of his hand on it and effectively imprisoning her. His eyes burned into hers with an intensity from which she couldn't look away. "I take exception to that accusation, which I am sure you didn't mean. You know your cousin better than I. Think on all I have said. You have nothing to lose and a great deal to gain."

She averted her eyes, tears streaming down her cheeks, and to her relief he backed away from her. "I beg your pardon for being so blunt with you."

"This is a very drastic form of revenge you propose, my lord."

"I have never been used so callously before. When you think on the matter yourself, you will own she has treated you with equal disdain."

"That still does not mean I am willing to throw in my lot with you."

"You'd be a fool not to."

"And if I fail in the task you set me?"

He shrugged his broad shoulders. "That is impossible, but whatever happens you will have gained so much.

Merely the act of parading you around the town on my arm will put her out of countenance. Think on it, Miss Trentham, and we will speak again on the morrow."

He leaned forward, and she almost flinched away, but he simply opened the door to let her out at last. She hesitated briefly and then, casting him one last look, fled to the solitude of her bedchamber.

Chapter Ten

The room Arabella had been assigned at Abbey Dulcis was the most comfortable she had ever occupied. Large and sumptuously furnished, it was quite a contrast to the modest chamber she occupied in her cousin's house. In fact, that was nothing more than a servant's room, even though she had the advantage of being the sole occupant, whereas servants were obliged to share.

Despite the comfort of her surroundings and her exhaustion, she found it difficult to sleep. She tossed and turned until at last she got up and went over to the window. Pulling back the curtain, she peered out into the unrelenting darkness, seeking some solace for her torment. She did believe Lord Carisbrooke when he said it wasn't Kitty who took her in. Her cousin did not possess a charitable bone in her body, but hearing it put so bluntly was hurtful, and for the first time since her father's demise Arabella felt resentment. Kitty had used and occasionally abused her. As Lord Carisbrooke had intimated, she could so easily have launched her into Society, although that would have utilized time and money her cousin would far rather spend on her own pleasures. It wasn't in her nature to assist another female to social prominence.

Even though Arabella had allowed an uncharacteristic bitterness to surface, she recognized she could never feel the anger and acrimony suffered by someone as proud as the marquess.

Considering his alarming proposal, she couldn't prevent herself dreaming of what it might be like to be Lady Carisbrooke. There was no doubt that whoever married the Marquess of Carisbrooke would be the subject of great interest in the beau monde. However, she was convinced even were she to be elevated to that position, she could never pose a threat to her cousin's standing as the Toast of the Town.

She sighed, for the lure of the scheme was undeniable, although she could certainly envisage the drawbacks, foremost being attracted to a man who saw her only as an instrument of revenge.

Her very thoughts added to her weariness, and with all those matters whirling about her brain, Arabella finally returned to her bed and succumbed to a no less troubled sleep. When a noise awoke her, she discovered it was daylight. Where she had left the curtains slightly open, sunlight streamed into the room, splashing across the counterpane like a stain. Puzzled by what had woken her, she slipped out of bed and padded across to the window. Her view was a pretty one, of the parterre and fountain and undulating fields spreading out as far as she could see.

For a few moments she couldn't discern what had disturbed her, and concluded it must have come from within the house. Then, when she was about to withdraw from the window, she heard the clatter of hooves just as the horse and rider came into view. Arabella had no notion of the time, but the marquess was fully dressed in the forest green coat with brass buttons. His legs, clad in tight-fitting pantaloons, hugged the flanks of his mount, which he contrived to control with the ease of a superb rider.

She heard him toss a laughing remark to an unseen groom and marveled at how relaxed he appeared for a man intent upon a course of revenge. At that moment she acknowledged he knew Kitty better than she liked to admit. He was aware of exactly what would injure his former lover most.

She continued to watch, unseen, at the window as he rode down the path toward the drive, a remarkably handsome man astride a magnificent horse. On many occasions, when he had visited Kitty in London, Arabella had observed him unseen from an upper window or landing, chiding herself for doing so, but unable to deny herself a covert look at him. He was the apogee of her hopeless dreams. It was so ironic that she should find herself in a position to achieve what she couldn't have possibly envisaged in her wildest imaginings a few days ago. Yet it would not be everything she dreamed of, a marriage based on a business agreement, but could she, Arabella asked herself, afford to turn down the only offer she was ever likely to receive, whatever the terms?

"Oh, Lucian," she said softly, using his name as often she did in the privacy of her own room in Berkeley Square.

Arabella continued to observe him until he was out of sight of the house, and then, turning away, she drew a profound sigh, but at last she had made up her mind. It only remained for her to inform Lord Carisbrooke of her decision.

Lord Loudon handed Lady Polstead down from his curricle, and after holding on to her gloved hand for longer than was absolutely necessary, he raised it to his lips.

"You must save for me the first waltz at Lady Spencer's rout," he whispered.

Kitty Polstead laughed delightedly. "I'm afraid I cannot, my lord. After all," she added eyeing him from beneath the brim of her bonnet, "you wouldn't wish to fuel any tattle, would you?"

The young man looked affronted. "Your integrity is of the greatest import to me. Unlike Carisbrooke, I would never be heedless of your situation." All at once he eyed her speculatively. "Tell me, my lady, is it true the great Corinthian left town because you gave him his turnips?"

Her delighted laugh rang around the square. "Oh, my dear, dear Loudon, you cannot possibly expect me to comment upon that. His lordship is entitled to keep a little of his pride intact."

"In my experience, *on dits* invariably contain a grain of truth."

"Again, I couldn't possibly say."

All at once the viscount frowned, noticing a mangy nag tied up by the railings. "Whose is that creature, do you think?"

"A peddler, perchance," Lady Polstead replied with a dismissive wave of her hand.

"It does not enhance your ladyship's abode one jot. If I were you, I would have it removed."

A few moments later, when she swept into the hall, she eagerly perused all the cards and invitations delivered in her absence, and in particular the little gifts of marchpane or flowers sent by admirers. The vexing disappearance of Lord Carisbrooke and her cousin had faded into the back of her mind, for there was so much more to look forward to, so many gentlemen eager to flatter and fawn upon her now that the marquess was no longer in close attendance. She'd been foolish to allow him to monopolize her to such an extent.

Her lips curved into a satisfied smile when she read one or two of the missives, and then a sound in the hall behind her caused her to turn to see her daughter standing a short distance away, her plain face set in a miserable expression.

How had she contrived to produce such an ill-favored child? Lady Polstead asked herself, but nevertheless managed to bestow a rare smile. "Hello, Molly. Why aren't you at your lessons?"

"I've finished for the day."

"Then, why don't you ask Miss Byford to take you for a walk? It would be far better for you than to hang around looking Friday-faced. You'll be casting me into the mopes."

"Mama, I really do miss Bella. Will she ever come back to us?"

Lady Polstead stiffened slightly at the mention of her cousin's name. "Naturally, dear, when she has finished nursing her aunt."

"She never mentioned any other relatives to me."

"No doubt she forgot."

"And I cannot conceive why she doesn't write to me. It is quite unlike Bella to be so heedless of us."

Her mother turned on her heel, saying through her teeth, "Molly, you are beginning to irritate me. Bella has only been gone a few days, and I have no way of knowing when our cousin will return. Perhaps we should prepare ourselves for the possibility she never will." As the child's face crumpled into near tears, her mother added, "Now, do go along and find Miss Byford. I don't know why I employ her if it is not to take charge of you."

Just at that moment the butler came into the hall. "My lady, his lordship asked that you go straight to the library when you return."

She threw down the handful of missives, scattering them across the floor. "Oh, this is outside of enough!"

While the lackey immediately stooped to pick them up, Lady Polstead turned her back on her tearful daughter and flounced up the stairs. When she entered the library, she immediately came face-to-face with a cadaverous-looking gentleman whose clothes were certainly not in the high kick of fashion and smelled distinctly of the stable.

She emitted a little squeal of alarm, and when her husband came forward, she demanded, "Who is this creature, Andrew? What is he doing in my house?"

He cleared his throat before answering in a constrained manner, "This . . . er . . . gentleman is Mr. Matthew Pike."

The fellow grinned at the fabled beauty, revealing a mouthful of blackened and broken teeth, something that caused her to shrink away before she sidled past him to put as much space between them as she could.

"What is he doing here? Tell him to go to the kitchen entrance."

"With a mother like you, it's no wonder the chit ran away," Pike responded.

"Mr. Pike was just about to leave," Sir Andrew broke in quickly. "He is . . . ah . . . the bearer of news, my dear, and if I interpret it correctly, it is of the most monumental, not to say disturbing, significance."

"What news can this tatterdemalion have for us?" her ladyship scoffed, turning away in the most pointed manner.

"I shouldn't have troubled myself if I'd known I'd get this ungrateful reception," the fellow whined.

"Perhaps you'd be kind enough to repeat what you told me, for the benefit of my wife before you go, Mr. Pike."

While the fellow fingered his greasy beaver hat resentfully, Lady Polstead went to the wall mirror and began to tuck in a few imagined stray hairs that might have been dislodged by her hat, turning this way and that to ascertain the perfection of her appearance.

"I was having a quiet drink at my local tavern, night

before last, when I was told by the landlord he had a runaway couple lodging there overnight . . ."

Her ladyship paused to glance at her husband. "Andrew, is this going to take much longer? My bath will be growing cold, and we are to attend Spencer House this evening."

"Just listen to this for a moment," her husband told her, and her face took on a look of mutinous resignation as she sank with practiced elegance into a wing chair. "Do continue, Mr. Pike."

"I got into conversation with the gentleman's servants who were drinking in the ordinary, and they told me they were in the service of the Marquess of Carisbrooke."

Once again, her ladyship started and then, having recovered herself quickly, she retorted, "What is this to us?"

"He was with a chit," Sir Andrew pointed out. "The servants seemed to believe she was connected to us. They heard her say on several occasions, with great emphasis apparently, that her name was Arabella Trentham."

Lady Polstead stared at her husband for several seconds before her head fell back against the chair. "I cannot conceive of this!"

"Saw them with my own glims," the fellow insisted in outraged tones. "Leastways, the landlord did."

"The jade!" she cried. "How could she do this to me? What does she think she's about?" Suddenly her eyes opened wide with shock. "*You* thought I was her *mother*!"

Her eyelids fluttered dangerously, and Sir Andrew snatched up his wife's fan and began to waft it to and fro in front of her face. "Now, now, my dear, no need to get into a pucker. Mr. . . . er . . . Pike hasn't good eyesight. Have you, Mr. Pike?"

"As good as the next man."

"Shall I send for your abigail, my dear? This has been the most dreadful shock to your nerves, and I fear they may have been badly overset."

"Just get that creature out of this house!"

Lady Polstead pushed the fan away and gripped the arms of the chair, fearful that the truth of the matter was about to come out. But what was the girl doing? she asked herself. No answer presented itself, only the unpalatable knowledge that the divine marquess and her plain, penniless, lackluster cousin had spent the night together. The news was well-nigh unbearable.

"She was supposed to be in Bath!" she protested, looking pained.

Sir Andrew hurriedly pushed a few coins across the desk in Matthew Pike's direction. "I'm obliged to you for the information, sir. I will deal with the matter from now on. You may go. We don't wish to clap eyes upon you again."

Matthew Pike snatched up the money and hurried to the door, where he cast Lady Polstead one last glance before he rushed out of the room.

"He thought I was her mother!"

"Stepmother, surely," Sir Andrew was quick to say as she drummed her heels on the floor. "He's evidently a lobcock . . . queer in the attic, but one must be obliged to him for the information. It is evident we have been cruelly deceived. Your cousin had no intention of going to Bath. She was eloping with Carisbrooke."

A moan escaped his wife's lips as he went on in an aggrieved tone, "This must have been going on beneath our very noses. I tell you, I am sorely disappointed in your cousin, Kitty."

"It was you who insisted on taking her in."

"I confess I was wrong, and you were right to resist

me. At the time it seemed to be the charitable thing to do. I had no notion she was such a slyboots."

"I always suspected it in her, although not to the precise degree. She always looks as if butter wouldn't melt in her mouth. Oh, it is beyond all bearing, Andrew!"

"What on earth can a man like Carisbrooke see in such a green girl, and why was the affair conducted in such secrecy? They are both eligible and neither under age."

Her ladyship groaned. "A man as proud as Carisbrooke wouldn't wish to be seen paying court to a penniless, not to say *plain* creature like my cousin, who is entirely without consequence. Instead he addressed himself to me, and I have not forgotten you castigated me for his attentions."

Sir Andrew looked pained. "Forgive me, Kitty my love. I have been a buffle-head, and I acknowledge it to you now with very great humility."

"The shock of it all is like to give me notice to quit." Lady Polstead slumped back into the chair once more.

Her husband clutched at her hand more tightly. "Oh, do not say so, dearest. The chit is not worth your megrims."

"She has betrayed our trust. She's an ingrate, a viper in my bosom. I doubt I shall ever recover from the treachery she has perpetrated with such deviousness."

"I've a mind to buy you a little gewgaw to make amends, not that I believe it can ever make up for such farouche behavior on your cousin's part."

"Nothing could."

"How would you like a little something from, say, Garrard's, my love?"

Lady Polstead was still furious with her cousin and the marquess, especially as she had no notion what they were up to. At least she had a very good excuse not to have Arabella back when she did eventually return, for whatever Matthew Pike had led them to believe, it was certain they had not eloped. The possibility that there was anything more than a night together under the one roof was out of the question, but she was happy enough to allow her husband to think there was.

When she looked up at him, it was with a pitiful smile she knew he could not resist. "I shall probably be obliged to consult Dr. Manfred without delay, so badly am I overset by this shock, but I daresay I might just be able to spare a little time to call in at the jeweler on the morrow to see if I can be diverted by a modest purchase."

With evident relief, he replied, "That's the barber! It would grieve me to see you down on yourself over this affair. You are usually as merry as a grig."

"Ah yes, but no one has ever subjected me to such Turkish treatment before."

His demeanor grew dark again, and as he moved away from her, he added, "I am going to pen a note to his lordship without another moment's delay, informing him of our outrage at his conduct in this matter. When they appear in London again, they had better be man and wife!"

Chapter Eleven

*A*fter Arabella had eaten a solitary meal in the breakfast room that overlooked the formal garden, there was still no sign of the marquess having returned from his ride. Resigned to having to wait, she began exploring Abbey Dulcis, which, although she had initially found the house daunting, discovered it had much to recommend it.

Mrs. Postlethwaite provided her with a pelisse and bonnet, Arabella having been obliged to leave Kitty's precious cloak behind at the inn, and although neither was particularly flattering to her, she was sufficiently accustomed to hand-me-down clothes and did not concern herself on that score.

Arabella wandered up and down the paths that bordered the formal beds in a desultory manner, alert all the while for any sign of the marquess's return. She explored the walled garden, skirted a maze, viewed the lake from a Grecian folly and then, when dark clouds threatened inclement weather, she returned to continue investigating the inside of the house.

For the first time she allowed herself to wonder about the rest of the Carisbrooke family. She speculated on whether she had ever heard mention of the cousin who was the master of Abbey Dulcis. The house was well run and luxurious, and it seemed evident there was a mistress to oversee its care. All at once Arabella realized that if she agreed to marry the marquess, she would become mistress of one of the loveliest houses in the land. A shiver ran down her spine at the very notion. However, she acknowledged wryly, if she did marry him, it would not be because he required a mistress for his country house. He only wanted someone to make Kitty jealous and regretful of her treatment of him. The notion that she should have this effect on the accomplished Lady Polstead was ludicrous, and if Lord Carisbrooke hadn't been so far gone in his lust for revenge, he would acknowledge it too.

All these thoughts and more milled through her mind as she wandered around the house, finding herself at last in the long gallery, which was lined with bookshelves filled with dusty tomes, and walls adorned by large portraits of ancestors. Arabella paused by each one in turn, eyeing them critically until she came to one of a youngish woman posing with a plain-looking baby on her knee. The style of the woman's clothing dated the portrait to about thirty years earlier, and there was something very familiar about her. Initially Arabella supposed it must be the late Lady Carisbrooke and her son, but the child, possessing thin lips and narrow eyes, bore no resemblance to the present marquess. Still, the feeling of recognition persisted until a noise at the far end of the gallery attracted her notice.

"Lord Carisbrooke?" she called, more anxious than ever to settle matters with him once and for all.

She rushed forward, only to slide to a standstill a few yards on, her heart starting to race even faster. Her face took on a look of abject horror. The moving figure was a monk whose arms were tucked into the sleeves of his habit, his tonsured head bowed in an appearance of piety. A score of gothic stories culled from novels borrowed from the circulating library leaped into her mind, blood-curdling tales that filled her mind with horror. A strangled cry rose up in her throat, but it was too dry to allow any sound to escape.

When the apparition disappeared from her sight, Arabella became mobile again. She turned on her heel and fled headlong in the opposite direction, only to come to an abrupt halt once more, this time at the head of the stairs when she saw the marquess coming toward her.

"Good morning, Miss . . ." he greeted her in the most urbane manner that seemed to Arabella at that moment totally inappropriate to the situation.

"You didn't tell me the house was haunted," she gasped, holding onto the newel post for fear she would fall.

He'd reached the landing, and his smile faded, a frown creasing his brow. "It isn't."

"Don't come the artful with me, my lord. I saw him."

"My dear young lady, you must be under the influence of an overactive imagination, or even the midsummer moon."

Her eyes grew wide. "I am not imagining it nor am I mad. I did see him! Just now. In the long gallery. A ghost. It was horrible."

He frowned again, peering at her as if her attic was to let. "What . . . kind of a . . . ghost did you see?"

She shuddered at the memory. "A monk . . ."

To her chagrin, he threw back his head and laughed. "That was no ghost!"

"I tell you I saw him! This house . . . it must be sited on the ruins of an old abbey . . ."

"So it is, and after the dissolution, Henry the Eighth gave the land to ancestors of my cousin."

"Then, the ghost I saw must be one of the monks who perished at the time of the dissolution. I tell you I did see him as clear as I am seeing you!"

The marquess put his hand on her arm in an attempt to calm her, only his touch had the opposite effect and caused her to tremble all the more. "What you saw was not an apparition. It was my cousin, Henry Brimston, who takes the family history to heart. Occasionally he secretes himself in a tower room to live like a monk for a while until he becomes bored and emerges again."

"Your cousin!" she gasped.

"I have an eccentric family."

"So I am beginning to understand."

"I'm very sorry you were alarmed. I should have warned you about him."

Arabella frowned and repeated. "Henry Brimston? Is he any relation to *Lady* Brimston?"

"His mother is my aunt."

"Lady Brimston," she repeated, realizing the portrait she had perused was of the young countess, now a very formidable matron of the ton, whose custom was to sail through fashionable diversions setting the most urbane socialites aquiver with her imperious manner and sharp tongue. "Perchance your cousin retreats to a monk's cell to escape his overbearing mama."

The marquess appeared momentarily startled by her observation, and then he began to laugh again. "How right you are! Cousin Henry might not be as cork-brained as I thought." When his laughter died away, he added, "You have a fine sense of humor, which is more than can be attributed to your cousin."

"So you are aware she has failings," she chided. "I was foolish enough to believe you considered her perfect."

"I never did. I was sensible of her shortcomings, more so than most. That is why I truly believed she would come with me to the Continent."

"Making such a mistake must be a rare fault in *you*."

"I perceived very quickly she had done me a service by her perfidious conduct."

"I cannot conceive why so eligible a gentleman pursued a married lady, when so many females who were entirely suitable threw themselves at your head."

"A huntsman derives far greater pleasure from the thrill of the chase than does his quarry."

Arabella smiled faintly. "I doubt if cousin Kitty would take kindly to being likened to vermin."

"Truth to tell," he admitted in a pensive tone, "I have never pursued the goal of marriage with great vigor."

"Much to the disappointment of so many."

"I couldn't see the sense in it."

"Not even to provide an heir for your considerable estates?" she asked with true curiosity.

"I don't care much for what comes after. My heir is a lawyer in Chichester, and he has several—I have lost count—children."

Taking a deep breath, Arabella told him, "Lord Carisbrooke, I cannot possibly marry you."

"Why not?" he asked in clipped tones.

"I could only marry for love."

"Balderdash!" he roared, making her flinch. "What utter nonsense you speak. Do you believe your cousin married for love? It would be plain to a blind idiot, she married Sir Andrew Polstead to ensure a comfortable future."

She drew herself up to full height, which didn't improve her stature above the diminutive. "Even so, my mind is made up."

"I have something that is like to change your mind in a brace of snaps," he told her, and taking her hand in his, he pulled her along the corridor.

Arabella had no choice but to trot in his wake until they reached a small study. Once the door was closed behind them, he took a sheet of parchment off the top of the desk and handed it to her. The seal was already broken, and Arabella unfolded it reluctantly, but the fine script only danced before her eyes.

"Oh, dear, I can't read it. My spectacles are still in London, where I left them."

He gasped with annoyance. "Don't tell me you are as blind as a beetle," he observed.

"I'm afraid I am considerably shortsighted," she told him, and he handed her his quizzing glass.

Carisbrooke,
Lady Polstead and I have just learned of your disgraceful behavior regarding our cousin. Having eloped with Miss Trentham, I trust you will do the honorable thing and not betray your origins as a gentleman, ensuring she returns to London your wife. If it should transpire that either of you are trifling, let me be categoric in insisting there is no longer any place for her in our lives.

Your servant,
Polstead

Arabella sank down into a chair, the note slipping from her nerveless fingers. "How did he hear about us?" she murmured to herself.

The marquess retrieved the missive and refolded it in two precise movements before replying, "It scarce matters."

"How did he know we were here?"

"He doesn't. The note was delivered to my London house and brought here this morning by one of my servants."

"I wonder what Kitty told him about my absence."

"Whatever it is, it's unlikely to be the truth. Shall we talk business now?"

She raised her eyes to meet his steel gray gaze, and shuddered at the coldness she saw there. "Do I have any option?"

"As I see it, none," was his uncompromising reply.

"I never have a choice. Everything in life is foisted onto me by others."

"This is not the time to wallow in self-pity," he told her, exhibiting not the slightest iota of sympathy.

"If it is not, I cannot conceive of another more timely."

"When you are Lady Carisbrooke, you will be your own mistress at last."

"My life will be orchestrated by you instead of Kitty. I shall merely exchange one form of bondage for another."

"Stuff and nonsense! What a tragedy queen you are! Your life will be infinitely better. It could scarce be worse."

Tears trembled on the tips of her lashes. "When you have recovered from this thirst for revenge, you will certainly hate me."

He gazed at her with a heartbreaking lack of passion. "My feelings for you are of no account. Now," he went on briskly, "let us discuss the fine details of the proposition. As you must have surmised, the offer is purely a business agreement. Nothing more, except that there will arise occasions in public when it will be politic to display a certain degree of affection for each other." He paused to subject her to a disconcerting stare before he added, "I'm persuaded that is not beyond your capabilities. Can you possibly manage to feign a degree of affection for me, Miss . . . Trentham?"

She forced herself to look at him, saying in a soft voice, "Oh yes, Lord Carisbrooke, I'm sure I can manage that very well indeed."

He crossed the room with very few strides, cupped her face between the palms of his hands, and before she had any chance to shy away, he kissed her roundly on the lips before drawing back again.

"That is what might be required of you."

Arabella touched her lips with a tentative finger. While her lips still tingled and her head continued to reel from the unexpectedness of the kiss and the pleasure it had given her, he began to move restlessly around the room. "You will, naturally, be accorded everything due my wife, both now and in the future," he added, swinging around to peer at her again. "When I am satisfied that Lady Polstead has been punished sufficiently, then we will gradually move to leading separate lives. It will not be perceived as anything out of the ordinary."

As he spoke, Arabella's eyes filled with tears yet again, and lest he noticed them, she turned to gaze unseeingly into the garden, visualizing the distant future when he deemed Kitty adequately chastened. No doubt she would be abandoned, alone and soon forgotten, to a handsome villa in Hans Town, with a carriage of her own and sufficient servants to meet her needs as befitting her station. That would be her reward for a task well-done. Neighbors would whisper that she was once the wife of the divine Marquess of Carisbrooke, and they would look at her and shake their heads in disbelief that he could ever have married such a colorless creature.

"Is that all acceptable to you?" he was asking, peering at her anxiously, and she nodded automatically.

"I had always envisaged, when I married, it would be for love," she answered, almost to herself, "with attendants and acquaintances present to share the happy occasion."

"That is romantical nonsense, Miss Trentham. Few marriages are contracted for such reasons, and those that are soon founder. You will be accorded great consequence and financial security. I doubt any female could wish for more."

"When is the wedding to take place?" she asked.

All at once Arabella was resolute. He expected her to shine. He required her to become the Toast of the Town. If it was at all possible, she would succeed brilliantly. If she failed—well he would abandon her all the sooner. It made no difference to the end result of this utter folly.

"I went this morning to procure a special license," he replied, shocking her anew. "And to engage Mr. Tomkins, the vicar of St. Saviour's, to conduct the proceedings. We can be married here in the chapel of Abbey Dulcis. I've arranged for Mr. Tomkins to attend us at six o'clock this evening."

Chapter Twelve

"*D*evil take it!" Henry Brimston gasped on hearing the news of his cousin's forthcoming nuptials. "I have been in retreat far too long if I am to emerge and discover you about to become leg-shackled."

The young man had discarded his monk's habit and now wore more traditional clothes befitting a country gentleman. His shaved tonsure gave him a comical appearance when worn with conventional garb. Seeing him at close quarters, Arabella could scarcely believe he was so close a relative of Lord Carisbrooke, for they bore no resemblance to one another, although she reminded herself that she and Kitty Polstead shared a similar connection and were entirely unalike. It was immediately evident that Lord Brimston was the baby in the portrait she had seen in the long gallery. He was still plain, his lips thin, but his nondescript appearance was belied by a pair of twinkling eyes. Arabella liked him from the start, and was relieved to discover he was nothing like the marquess or, indeed, his fearsome mother, who she had frequently observed reducing sophisticated ladies into a quivering mass of nerves with a few choice words.

"It's opportune you're here, Monk," the marquess informed his cousin, "for you can stand up for me."

"Delighted."

When he glanced again at Arabella, there was clearly a

glint of curiosity present in his eyes. She didn't blame him, for she was hardly the kind of handsome female with whom Lord Carisbrooke usually kept company. She was still clothed in the grubby and torn gown she'd worn to shin down from the inn window, so she couldn't even present a picture of elegance—and she was certainly no picture-book bride.

"I have it in mind this decision to marry is a sudden one," Lord Brimston ventured.

"It's a long story," his cousin explained hastily, and then, glancing out of the window, added with a good deal of relief, "I believe Mr. Tomkins has arrived."

Arabella drew in a sharp breath. There was still time to cry off, but she knew she would not. Now Sir Andrew was aware she was with the marquess, she could never return to Polstead House, and there was certainly nowhere else she could go if she chose not to become Lady Carisbrooke. Ironically, there were a score of debutantes who would have gladly changed places with her at that moment.

The two men started across the room, leaving Arabella where she stood, almost paralyzed with fear. When they reached the door, they realized she was not with them, and the marquess paused to glance back at her.

"Are you coming or not?" he asked without troubling to hide his exasperation.

There followed an infinitesimal pause before she went to join them, a strangely mute and somber wedding party.

"Ah, the bride!" exclaimed Mr. Tomkins on entering the house.

Arabella was impressed by his ability to remain nonplussed when faced with a hasty marriage to perform and a bride who looked like a tatterdemalion. The strange wedding party moved quickly in the direction of the chapel to be met there by the butler and housekeeper, who had been engaged to bear witness to the proceedings.

The atmosphere was entirely unreal to Arabella as she took her place at the marquess's side in front of the altar. This could have been the culmination of all her impossible hopes; instead it was a nightmare. She could almost believe she would soon be wakened by Molly jumping on her bed in Polstead House, and find herself laughing at her own stupid dreams.

"I now pronounce you man and wife," the vicar intoned, beaming at the couple.

Arabella dared to look at her husband for the first time since the ceremony began, but instead of giving her the smile of reassurance she craved, his face might have been chiseled out of stone. A moment later he turned woodenly on his heel and marched out of the chapel.

All the others watched him go, obviously mystified by his behavior. A heavy silence hung over them all as each searched for something appropriate to say.

Lord Brimston was the first to recover, taking her hand and bowing over it. "Let me be the first to wish you happy, Lady Carisbrooke."

Lady Carisbrooke! The reality of her new station hit Arabella like a mailed fist. She was actually married to the divine marquess, and yet it was no marriage at all.

"My lady, I need his lordship to sign the parish register," Mr. Tomkins told her in dismay.

"It's the emotion of the moment," she blurted out. "His lordship is very much affected by it. You will be obliged to excuse him his behavior."

She noted Lord Brimston's smile of approval, and added, "If you'll be so good as to leave the register with me, I will make sure it is signed and returned to St. Savior's."

The vicar continued to appear concerned until Postlethwaite offered, "Allow me to provide you with refreshment before you leave, sir."

He nodded to Arabella and Lord Brimston, who whispered, "You were magnificent, my dear. I don't know what all this signifies, but I wager you'll make a very good match for my cousin."

She sketched a curtsy before replying, "By your leave, my lord. I believe I must have words with my ..." she faltered before adding in a strangled voice, "my husband."

Postlethwaite directed her toward Lord Carisbrooke's study and she burst in without so much as a knock. The marquess had been standing by the window, staring out into the garden and, Arabella didn't doubt, regretting his impetuous wedding.

"If you regret what has just transpired, you can seek an immediate annulment," she said the moment she entered the room.

"No," he answered without hesitation.

She slammed the tome down on the desk, saying, "Then, you'd better sign the parish register."

"Leave it, and I'll attend to the matter," he answered, turning back to the window in a manner that was both dismissive and infuriating.

"Is that all you have to say to me?"

"What else is there to say?" was his indifferent reply.

"Lucian, how could you possibly leave me at the altar?" she asked, and he turned to look at her once again, appearing mildly surprised at the use of his given name.

"I understood the ceremony had concluded. You'd have more cause for complaint had I left you before the service took place."

Arabella choked back her anger, saying softly, "You expect certain duties from me that I have agreed against good sense to fulfill, but in return I demand respect from you."

"You have it."

"No, I think not. Your behavior just now proves the point."

"We've been leg-shackled only minutes, and you've already turned into a shrew."

"I entered into this farce of a marriage with extreme reluctance and deep foreboding. If you continue to treat me with this degree of contempt, I shall be obliged to leave, and you cannot prevent me from doing so indefinitely."

He smiled at last. "There's no need to be tongue-valiant, my dear. You have nowhere else to go now."

"Don't be so certain of that!"

"Surely you're not contemplating throwing yourself on your cousin's charity. You know full well she will not welcome you, especially now you have a new appendage to your name. She can hardly use the Marchioness of Carisbrooke as her unpaid servant."

Stung by his amusement, she retorted, "I no longer need to rely upon my cousin's largesse. I could easily obtain a position as a governess."

"Without a letter of recommendation? I doubt you'd get far unless you are relying upon me to furnish you with one."

"The name of Lady Carisbrooke would be recommendation enough to some city mushroom eager to elevate himself further."

He took out his gold hunter and glanced at it briefly before returning it to his pocket. "Well, Arabella, my dear, we have been leg-shackled for less than thirty minutes, and you already have me at a stand."

She didn't quite trust the mellow note in his voice, but nevertheless prompted, "So you will in future treat me with at least basic civility?"

103

"I will deal with you far better than that; it will be a pleasure to act the doting bridegroom to my adoring bride." She cast him a disbelieving look as he came around the desk and gazed at her somberly. "I wonder if I've taken on more than I anticipated," he murmured, raising her chin with one finger and gazing deep into her eyes.

Arabella twisted away from his touch, for she couldn't trust her own reaction to that degree of intimacy. "It would serve you right if you had," she told him, her voice uneven beneath his dark scrutiny.

All at once he smiled, causing her heart to flutter. "But we'll certainly have fun exacting our revenge, won't we, Belle?"

Using a diminutive form of her name had a profound effect upon her. She swallowed noisily, and her legs became suddenly weak. Unaware of his influence over her emotions, the marquess offered her his arm. "Let's go and take dinner with Monk, and drink a toast to our future."

There isn't one, she wanted to protest, but instead she linked her arm with his and allowed him to escort her out of the room.

Chapter Thirteen

"*I* note the Czar of Russia and the King of Prussia will be coming to London to celebrate the victory over Boney," Lord Brimston remarked as he read his newspaper during breakfast.

Arabella had been toying with a piece of bread and butter, but now she looked up at her new relative and feigned an interest.

"I imagine there will be great festivities."

"Prinny is bound to orchestrate the most vulgar display." Arabella chuckled her agreement as Lord Brimston went on to ask, "Does Carisbrooke intend to go up to London?"

"Yes, as soon as I've been furnished with suitable clothing," she answered, having been told that much herself. "Carisbrooke has engaged a local dressmaker to run up a few items to tide me over."

"Once you're ensconced in Grosvenor Square, he'll seek out tradespeople of the finest repute to supply you with all you require, for chaw-bacon styles aren't likely to make Lady Polstead smoky."

Arabella sighed. "So he's told you about that."

"And I admonished him in no uncertain terms, my dear. This scheme is exceedingly crack-brained to put it mildly." He paused to peer at her myopically across the table. "Do you share his taste for revenge, my lady?"

The use of her new title still took her aback somewhat, but she was learning not to show it. "I've never considered myself a vengeful person, but as my future security is so uncertain, I have no alternative but to go along with his lordship's plans, foolish as I believe them to be. My cousin might be miffed when she hears of my marriage, but that won't last for long. In truth, Lord Brimston, there is no possible chance of my becoming the Toast of the Town. I'm no beauty, and I have neither wit nor style to recommend me."

Henry Brimston glanced up at her. "My dear, you do yourself great disservice." She felt her cheeks growing pink as the young man added, "Let me warn you to accustom yourself to receiving compliments of that kind. You'll be subjected to a great many once you come out into Society, as well as the earnest attentions of toad-eaters anxious to grease your boots."

She laughed, shaking her head in disbelief. "Oh, my dear Lord Brimston, I cannot conceive of that."

Arabella was still laughing merrily when her husband came in dressed for riding and carrying a whip. He cocked his head to one side, saying, "My cousin is evidently keeping you amused."

"On the contrary, my dear fellow, Lady Carisbrooke is the most diverting company I have ever had the privilege to enjoy." He jumped to his feet, hastily dabbing his lips with his napkin. "I beg you both excuse me: I have estate business to attend."

The moment he had left the room, Arabella immediately became shy under the marquess's intense scrutiny. He was seeking some redeeming feature in her, she thought, and could find none.

"I've come to give you a lesson in carriage driving."

"Do I need one?" she asked, feeling nonplussed.

"Indeed—if you are to cut a dash. I have ordered a

racing curricle for you. It will be very splendid, and I expect you to drive to an inch. In the meantime you can practice on Brimston's rather less than prime carriage."

"I'm afraid you expect a good deal of me."

"I believe I have already made you sensible of that fact. Come along, Belle, we've no time to lose." He strode toward the door with Arabella following less keenly. "You have a lot to learn in a very short time. Now there are to be Allied festivities in London, we'll have to be in the forefront of the diversions. My house is perfect for holding grand balls and soirees."

Arabella's progress came to an abrupt halt on the threshold of the house. "Let me be clear on the matter, Lucian. Are you saying I will be obliged to host balls and other diversions for the entertainment of royalty?"

"Naturally. If you are to be socially prominent, all those who are of any consequence must be invited to our soirees. Of our own royal family, only Prinny will need to be issued with an invitation, as His Majesty is now confined to Windsor by his madness."

"You are no less queer in the attic and could easily join His Majesty at Windsor. I couldn't poss—"

He took her arm and guided her down the steps to where Henry Brimston's rather shabby curricle was standing. "You'll contrive handsomely, my dear. Here, let me help you onto the box."

When he climbed up beside her, she said in a bemused voice, "You have told me little of what is expected of me, save being obliged to endure your embrace when the circumstances warrant it."

He turned to smile at her. "Endure, Belle? You'll positively enjoy it, I promise."

She drew in a sharp breath as he climbed up on the box beside her. "You are so puffed up with your own consequence, I find it intolerable."

107

"Your attitude toward me is immaterial, and if you have observed your cousin to any degree, you will know very well how to go on."

"Ha!" she scoffed. "Now you wish me to emulate cousin Kitty!"

"I don't want to suggest you pattern yourself on her in all ways, just in the manner she conducts her *social* life. I know you understand very well what I mean, so don't stand on points."

"You must first of all tell me what I am to expect in your London house."

"It's situated in Grosvenor Square and said to be the largest town house in London." On hearing her groan, he took up the ribbons and set the team in motion. "Does that daunt you?"

"Yes. It most certainly does."

Maddeningly he answered, "I have every faith in your abilities. It's just that you've never had the opportunity to shine before. Your cousin has always cast a shadow over your existence, which I own is not so surprising. Once you are mistress of your own establishment, I believe you will contrive very well indeed."

"I'll certainly do my best."

He glanced at her, and she couldn't mistake the steely tone of his voice. "You'll do better than that—you'll succeed brilliantly. Remember, it's better to be mistress of your own establishment than dogsbody in that of your cousin's."

They'd been traveling at a leisurely pace up the carriage drive of Abbey Dulcis, the horses responding to the slightest movement of the ribbons. As during their escape from the inn, Arabella was forced to admire his skill in handling the team. They drove through the towering gates and onto the road beyond, whereupon he told her, "Time for you to take over, Belle."

"I would far rather observe you for a little longer."

"Don't be hen-hearted," he teased.

Her hands were trembling when she took control of the curricle, and then to an even greater extent as he moved closer on the box, slipping one arm around her to help guide her movements.

"That's fine," he murmured, his lips uncomfortably close to her ear. "Be gentle with them, and they'll respond to your every command."

"What a pity you don't employ tender tactics when you're dealing with females," she retorted.

The marquess drew away from her, causing the team to lunge forward. He immediately put his arm around her again, quickly restoring a rhythm to their movements. Arabella allowed herself to sink back against him, enjoying his strength and reveling in his manly power.

At length he withdrew again, saying in an unusually muted tone, "See how quickly you learn."

She laughed harshly. "Coming from a nonesuch, that is praise indeed."

He took his gold hunter out of his pocket and sprung open the cover. "Turn the curricle 'round, Belle. It's time to go back."

His order caused her a frisson of disappointment, and belatedly she came to understand she'd actually been enjoying herself. "Must we?"

"I'm afraid so. I've engaged a caper-merchant to come in and give you some dancing lessons."

"I can dance!"

"We'll see how well," he answered, before showing her how to turn the curricle around without tipping it over in the process.

To her dismay, he insisted on remaining in the ballroom to watch the dancing lessons take place. Try as she would to ignore him, Arabella was very much aware of his presence, just as she always had been, even in a room holding hundreds of people. The effect was to render her clumsy, and both the teacher and the marquess soon became impatient with her.

"I don't believe I can do this while you're watching me, Lucian," she told him.

"Remember, hundreds of people will be observing you with very great interest when we are in London."

She shivered with apprehension at so timely a reminder, but did renew her efforts to concentrate on the steps. Even with little experience, she executed them better in London.

Finally her husband threw down the stick he had been using to mark time, and declared, "Let me partner my wife, sir, and we'll see then if that makes a difference."

"That will only serve to make me more nervous," she protested.

"Stuff and nonsense! I'm not an ogre."

"Well, I'm beginning to believe you are," she retorted angrily, standing with her hands on her hips.

"If that is what you truly think of me, what opinion can you have of Lady Polstead?"

"Evidently not as adoring as yours!"

"Lord and Lady Carisbrooke! I beg of you!" the dancing master protested. "I cannot possibly continue tutoring her ladyship without some sense of decorum."

While Arabella glared at her husband, the marquess, surprisingly, appeared contrite. "I do beg your pardon, sir. My wife is now ready to attend you." Before she could object further, he grabbed her around the waist, pulled her against him, and said, "She has little experience of dancing the waltz. We'll concentrate on that for the remainder of the afternoon."

Lord Brimston discovered her crying on a bench in the formal garden long after the dancing master had left and the marquess had returned to the study. "Now, now, my dear, what on earth is troubling you?"

"Your cousin, naturally. He's an odious, overbearing, toplofty man, with no feelings whatsoever. I was a fool to allow him to browbeat me into this marriage, which is nothing but a farce in any event. I'm horribly miserable, my lord, and have no notion what to do about it."

"Call me, Monk—everyone does," he invited as he sat down beside her and handed her his lace-edged handkerchief.

She accepted it gratefully and then half turned away from him, ashamed of her own lack of control and red-rimmed eyes. It was a sad omen of what would happen once they were residing in London.

"We are cousins after all, and I can assure you Carisbrooke is not the beast you consider him. I know he's impatient and can be impetuous, otherwise this situation would never have arisen, but at heart he is a good fellow, and you will emerge from this situation accomplished in many areas."

"He's schooling me just to miff my cousin. When he is done with me, such social graces won't be much use. The nub is, I don't care about Kitty overmuch; whether she's in a tweak over our marriage or not is no concern of mine."

"What *do* you care about, my dear?" he asked in a gentle voice.

She didn't answer for a moment or two. She just twisted the handkerchief around in her fingers. "Lucian. My regard for him is more than I care to confess."

"I know *that*, my dear."

Arabella turned to him then, her moist eyes wide with alarm. "You *know*, Monk?"

He smiled apologetically. "I'm afraid it is transparently obvious to me."

111

"Do you suppose Lucian is also aware of it?" she asked in a voice that was lowered into a horrified whisper.

"Probably not. Why don't you tell him?"

She drew back in alarm. "Oh no, I cannot! I know he has no regard for me, and any confession on my part will only induce him to despise me. And you must not. Vow to me, Monk, you won't tell him!"

"No need to get into a pucker, my dear. Your secret is safe with me, but I'm bound to confess, for the first time in his life I believe the fellow's fit for Bedlam. I've met Lady Polstead and declare she cannot hold a candle to *you*."

Arabella laughed and impulsively threw her arms around his neck, kissing his cheek. "You are such a dear, Monk."

After a moment he drew away, saying with uncharacteristic seriousness, "Carisbrooke is the luckiest man in the world to have you as his wife, and the shame is he isn't even aware of it."

The sound of footsteps induced them both to look up to see the marquess standing a few yards away, his expression unrelievedly grim as he observed the light-hearted intimacy between his wife and his cousin.

"The mantua-maker has arrived to fit your clothes. I thought you ought to know."

Arabella jumped to her feet and smoothed down her gown. She cast Lord Brimston one last apologetic glance before joining her husband and saying, "It will be a relief to have a change of clothing."

He started to walk back in the direction of the house, and she was hard-pressed to keep up with his long-legged and determined stride. He didn't appear to notice signs of her recent distress, and in the face of his tight-lipped demeanor, she ventured, "Your cousin is being most kind to me, Lucian."

"So I noticed."

"He has tendered a good deal of valuable advice, which will stand me in good stead when we go up to London."

He laughed without mirth as he opened the door for her. "Fond as I am of my cousin, he is not in the least worldly or stylish and, therefore, there is little counsel Monk could furnish that would be of use to you."

"That is a harsh and unwarranted thing to say," she protested.

"It is nevertheless true, and I commend you very strongly to consider the wisdom of behaving in such a hoydenish manner with any gentleman who is not your husband, for it is like to be misinterpreted by those eager to spread *on dits*."

"It's evident you have misconstrued my gratitude for your cousin's kindness to me," she answered heatedly. "It is not in the least justified."

"Very possibly, but it still remains that the only person to whom you should direct your affection is your new husband."

"I find that very difficult indeed."

"I'm aware of it."

"Perhaps if you showed the slightest sign of affection toward me, it would be easier," she ventured, glancing at him uncertainly.

It was immediately evident she had disconcerted him. Unthinkingly she had allowed him to escort her to the drawing room, where he paused to say, "I had Mrs. McFee shown in here."

She struggled to contain her emotions and murmured in the manner of a farewell. "Thank you, Lucian."

To her dismay he insisted upon accompanying her inside. "You won't mind if I remain to inspect the clothes you have made for her ladyship," he informed, rather than asked, the startled mantua-maker.

The woman glanced at Arabella before replying, "This is most . . . unusual, my lord."

"I daresay" was the only comment he made before he settled himself into a chair, thrusting his long legs out in front of him. Then, with a wave of his hand, he ordered, "Get on with it. I haven't got all day to spend on such matters."

The dressmaker appeared considerably put out by his manner. Nevertheless she ushered Arabella to a screen behind which she fitted her into several garments. They were then shown to Lord Carisbrooke, who nodded his approval. All the while his demeanor indicated he remained in a foul temper, and Arabella was puzzled as to what had induced his ill humor. Certainly not seeing her enjoying Henry Brimston's company, she was sure.

To Arabella, the few garments ordered were the most beautiful she had ever worn, although from all she had observed in her cousin's house, they were not in the first stare of fashion. Nevertheless, she was delighted to have something to wear other than her own torn muslin, and the outmoded evening gown produced for her by Mrs Postlethwaite.

"Do you approve?" Arabella couldn't resist asking when she showed him the chintz day dress that needed no further alteration.

He examined her slowly, and with such thoroughness her cheeks flamed with embarrassment. At length he conceded, in a voice low enough to escape the dressmaker's hearing, "It will serve until we reach London. You have a fine figure. It's a great pity your cousin saw fit to provide you only with the most outmoded and unflattering garments."

"Oh . . ." Arabella replied in dismay, not knowing whether she should be pleased at his praise or wounded by his criticism.

"I trust the garments meet with your ladyship's approval," the woman said, and added pointedly, "and your lordship's."

"Yes, indeed," he answered with no enthusiasm.

"*I* am delighted," Arabella added pointedly.

As the woman backed away toward the door, she said unsmilingly, "I shall have these back as soon as possible, my lady."

"Treat it as a matter of urgency," the marquess told her, and then as the door closed behind her, he said to Arabella, "Anyone would imagine I had never clapped eyes on a female in her petticoats before."

"Not this female," she reminded him, and when she moved away, he reached out to draw her back toward him.

Startled, Arabella looked up into his eyes, which just then were filled with a dark passion that caused something to stir inside her. She knew immediately what it was—love. Despite all that had happened between them, learning he was not the perfect hero of her unrequited dreams had done nothing to diminish something that had quietly fomented every time he appeared at Polstead House.

"In view of our unusual marital arrangement, I am prepared to allow you considerable license in your behavior, Belle, but don't, I warn you, seek to emulate your cousin's laxity in that province, for you'll discover that displeases me greatly. A substantial degree of rectitude is demanded of you. Do you understand?"

She was unable to tear her gaze away from his fierce

one, and then, when she nodded slowly, it was the marquess who released his grip on her arm and finally walked away, leaving her frustrated and prey to feelings she couldn't possibly express.

Chapter Fourteen

"*It*'s time to see how well you can handle a horse," Lucian told Arabella when he encountered her in the hall a few days later.

Mercifully his ill humor had disappeared, but all the same she complained, "I can ride perfectly well, Lucian."

"You said you could dance, but it has taken several lessons to perfect your ability."

"Only the waltz. I had no experience of that."

"You're too hard on her ladyship," Lord Brimston commented as he passed through the hall with his land steward.

"My wife lived with Lady Polstead, so she is used to harsh treatment," the marquess countered, something that made her smile.

"I sometimes think she was kind compared to you."

"Then, I'll begin to order you to run useless errands for me," he countered.

"As long as you don't require me to deliver your billets-doux." His face darkened, and Arabella immediately regretted her trite remark. "I don't have a riding habit," she added quickly.

"I've instructed Mrs. Postlethwaite to find one of Lady Brimston's and put it out for you. I'm sure you'll find she has done so by now."

Arabella's eyes grew round. "Lady Brimston! She's huge."

"She was once as slight as you." He tapped her lightly on the behind with his riding whip. "Run along and change now, Belle. I'll wait right here for you to return."

"So you don't intend to supervise my change of clothing," she retorted, alluding to his presence the other day when she tried on her new gowns.

"Only if you insist," was his rejoinder as she ran up the stairs, fearful that he might take her literally.

It was difficult to believe that Lady Brimston was once able to wear the slim-fitting riding habit, but when Arabella saw her reflection in the mirror, she was not displeased with the effect it had on her appearance. The darkness of the material highlighted the flawless fairness of her complexion and brightened the color of her hair. The set of the hat seemed to enhance the size of her eyes, making them appear to be an even deeper green. For the first time she began to suspect the dowdy, outmoded clothes she'd always been obliged to wear had made her seem plain, while the looking glass inferred something quite different was the truth.

Her heart was beating unaccountably fast when she came down to join him. He was reading through some letters that had arrived, but when he heard her footsteps on the stairs, he turned around on his heel and stared at her for what seemed to be a very long time. Arabella's cheeks grew warm beneath the veil of her hat, and she was forced to avert her eyes.

At length he said, rather abruptly, "You see, it does fit. Well, come along, Belle. Don't hang in the hedge. We have much work to do."

"In truth, I had never considered marriage a job of work," she told him airily while they walked to the stables.

118

He cast her a sidelong glance. "No doubt, you never thought of marriage at all."

Stung by the reminder, she retorted, "You are quite wrong. I had every hope of it."

To her satisfaction, his eyebrows rose in surprise. "Then, I beg your pardon for the error. Am I acquainted with the fortunate gentleman?"

"Lord Redesby expressed a decided interest in me."

His scornful laughter mortified her. "How flattering for you! He's old enough to be your grandfather. He has outlived two wives and enjoyed countless Cyprians, but to date has produced no heir. That I suppose was going to be your task."

Arabella gasped. "Am I supposed to be flattered by the terms of *this* marriage, Lucian? It might have been an odd match with Lord Redesby, but this is no match at all."

His eyes narrowed as he observed her with a detachment she had come to hate. "Why on earth did I consider you suitably submissive?" he asked of no one in particular, in a vexed tone of voice that a short time earlier would have worried her.

"Simply because you didn't take the trouble to know me."

They had come to the stable yard, where two handsome horses were awaiting their arrival. Arabella marched up to the one bearing a sidesaddle, but before the stable boy could help her mount, the marquess had moved him aside.

"Don't get on your high ropes, Belle," he advised. He lifted her easily into the saddle, and as he did so he asked softly, "Am I to take it you would like to alter the terms of our marriage agreement?"

Arabella was so startled, she slid right out of the saddle and would have fallen to the ground if he hadn't caught her in his arms. Her initial cry of alarm was cut short by so soft a landing, but a moment later she was discomforted anew by being held against him and the intensity of his expression as he gazed down at her. Her heart beat fast as his lips hovered close to hers. His eyes burned darkly. But then without warning, his expression changed. The intensity disappeared.

"Why, Belle!" he exclaimed while she remained ensconced in his strong arms, startling her out of her heady feelings. "I had no notion you possessed green eyes. You'll carry the Carisbrooke emeralds very well indeed."

Surprised by his statement and diverted from her discomfiture, she asked, "Are they larger and finer than the Polstead sapphires?"

"Much," he answered and, unable to help herself, she buried her face in his shoulder, laughing merrily until he placed her gently back in the saddle a few moments later.

When they rode out of the stable yard, he informed her, "As soon as all your new clothes are delivered, we can go back to town."

She cast him a horrified look. Although she had known from the outset this was his intention, the reminder was an unwelcome one, and she rode ahead so he should not be aware of her unease.

"At least you were correct about being able to ride," he called after her. "You have an excellent seat."

"You admired my figure and complimented my seat. I wonder what might come next."

She dug in her heels, and as the horse responded, Lucian galloped alongside. "By the by, I've arranged for the announcement of our marriage to appear in all the influential journals, to coincide with our return to London."

Roaring with laughter at her shocked expression, he

dug in his spurs and galloped ahead of her, leaving Arabella to consider the consequences of what he had done.

The servants formed an uneasy group, standing outside Lady Polstead's boudoir, glancing at each other with nervous stares while listening intently to the noise emanating from within.

"She's boxed my ears," Temple protested tearfully when she emerged, followed by a volley of invective from within. "All I did was deliver a note that had arrived for her ladyship this morning, nothing more."

Molly Polstead had joined the worried crowd and looked no less concerned, until her father marched up the stairs and the servants melted away, save for the one footman on duty.

"Papa, Mama is truly distempered this morning," the child told him.

"So I hear," he answered grimly as the sound of a further crash reached his ears.

"What can have put her on her high ropes?"

"I have a vague suspicion. Stay here, Molly, and I will deal with your Mama." He straightened up and nodded to the footman who successfully concealed his amusement and leaned forward to open the door. The moment he did so a cushion came sailing out of the room, whistling past Sir Andrew's ear and over the banister rail to bounce off the house steward's head.

Sir Andrew checked and then plunged into the boudoir to face his distraught wife, who was still wearing a silk wrap with her hair falling haphazardly around her face.

"So you've read the *Morning Post*," he said without preamble, eyeing the scene of carnage before him.

In her temper Lady Polstead had strewn furnishings about the room and shards of glass and fragments of china littered the floor. The full-length mirror, normally a prominent part of his wife's life, lay on its side, a mass of splintered glass.

"He's married her, Polstead! That little nobody has inveigled him in some way to make her his wife. Oh, the humiliation. I shall be a laughingstock! How shall I bear it?"

"With dignity, naturally. Indeed, it cannot be a disadvantage to be related to the Carisbrookes." When she howled with rage, he added hastily, "You ought to be pleased."

Kitty Polstead stared at him aghast, her face pale. "Pleased! Why should it please me? He's made a fool of me, pretending to admire me and then running off with *her*. I tell you it's past all bearing."

"I beg of you, dearest, don't fly up into the boughs. Continue in this vein, and you're like to have a seizure."

"I am already suffering the most agonizing palpitations and spasms."

"Allow me to send for Dr. Mercer."

Ignoring him, Lady Polstead snatched up a letter from a drum table and brandished it in the air. "That creature has had the temerity to write to me, Polstead. Can you conceive of her being so bumptious?"

"Kitty . . ."

"She has the effrontery to hope we will remain friends and signs herself Lady Carisbrooke in the knowledge it is like to make an end of me!"

"Lady Carisbrooke is her name," Sir Andrew pointed out, not unreasonably, but his attempts to calm his wife only resulted in her shrieking loudly as she shredded the offending letter and consigned it to the fire.

"She's no longer our responsibility, Kitty, and it has cost us nothing to see her so well settled. That, surely, is a great blessing."

Lady Polstead wrapped her arms around her shaking

body. "All that concerns you is parsimony when this farce of a marriage has cost me dear."

"You exaggerate."

"You have no conception of the consequences. I am betrayed by my own cousin."

"Balderdash!"

Her response to his scorn was to utter a shrill and prolonged scream. Sir Andrew marched across the room and struck her sharply on the cheek, thus arresting the outburst. His wife's eyes opened wide with shock as he took hold of both her arms.

"I trust this attack of the vapors is not prompted by your affection for that fribble."

"Polstead! How can you suggest such a thing?" she protested before gasping, going rigid, then falling limply onto the sofa.

Sir Andrew was immediately contrite. "Kitty, Kitty. Oh, my love, what have I done?" There was no response, and then, on seeing a pale face at the door, called to his daughter, "Send for Temple! Tell her to burn feathers! Your mama has swooned!" Then he began to chafe his wife's hand. "Kitty, I didn't mean it. You know I didn't. Kitty, I beg your pardon, my love. I know how fond you are of Arabella, but you'll be obliged to harden your heart to that ingrate."

Her eyes fluttered open. "As long as you do not turn against me, my dear."

"Never, Kitty! I adore you. You know I do. I vow I will make amends for this hurt that has smote your kindly heart. You took her in and lavished her with kindness and generosity, and betrayal has been your reward. I shall go this very morning to Garrard's to purchase their finest diadem for you. That will surely raise your spirits."

She sighed. "So kind, so thoughtful as always, but

123

even so generous a gesture on your part won't make up for the heartache I have suffered on that chit's account."

Temple came rushing into the room, and Sir Andrew straightened up, telling the woman, "Attend your mistress. I must go to Bond Street, but I'll be back in a trice, Kitty, never you fear."

When the door closed behind Sir Andrew, Temple attempted to hold a vinaigrette under her mistress's nose, but Lady Polstead stood up, rudely brushing her abigail aside.

"Don't trouble yourself with that nonsense, Temple. Fetch me some slices of cucumber for my eyes and lemon juice for my skin. Then you will help me dress. I must go to consult Dr. Manfred with no further delay. I have no Oil of Amaranthe left, and I need it desperately if that bread-and-butter miss isn't to cast me into oblivion!"

Lord Carisbrooke waited with scarce concealed impatience in the hall of Brimston House until he was ushered into his aunt's drawing room. The heavy brocade curtains were drawn across the windows, allowing in only a modicum of light. The awesome countess could only just be distinguished—a large mound reclining on a daybed, a vinaigrette clutched in one hand. The table drawn up at her side was plentifully supplied with sweetmeats—marchpane and sugarplums in particular.

"Aunt Ernestine?" the marquess ventured when he was a few paces from the daybed.

"So you have deigned to call upon your old aunt at last," was her reply.

He smiled faintly. The strength of her voice belied the weakness of her pose. "I have been out of town for a while."

"That is not an excuse."

"No, but surely it must be held to be a reason."

"Oh, it's so terrible to be old and unwanted. My one surviving nephew—my only son."

"Stuff and nonsense, Aunt," he scoffed as he drew up a chair and sat down. "No one enjoys so diverse a social life as you. As for your son—he declares his intention of following me to London."

The countess raised her head at last. The prevailing fashion for flimsy figure-hugging gowns in the classical style did nothing to flatter her bulky figure.

"Brimston is coming to town? I cannot conceive of that."

"He was attracted by the prospect of all the victory celebrations about to take place."

"I'm sure it wouldn't be on account of his ailing mother."

"Aunt Ernestine, did you receive my note?"

"I did, and I have since read the announcement in the *Post*. Indeed, I wish you both happy. Naturally, I was the last to hear of your marriage, not that it surprises me. . . ."

"Aunt, you are the first to know of it with the exception of Monk, who happened to be at Abbey Dulcis when the marriage took place."

"Don't call Brimston by that ridiculous name. It only encourages him in his foolishness."

With a wry smile her nephew said, "Beg pardon, Aunt."

"Everyone is talking about this marriage of yours, I'll have you know."

"That doesn't surprise me in the least," was his satisfied reply.

"The tattle is endless, and I am in no position to comment, which, as you might imagine, is most vexing. The *on dits* are ever more fanciful."

"It's just as well we're back in town, then."

"I just don't understand what has prompted you to be

125

so rash. When I saw you not a sennight ago, you were dancing attendance on Kitty Polstead as if she was the last female left in the world."

"Everyone dances attendance on Kitty Polstead," he answered, hoping his aunt would not discern his discomfiture. "She takes a pet if one does not."

Lady Brimston's eyes narrowed. "You've been as close as oak over this girl, and it's not at all like you. Naturally, you are ever disobliging in such matters. Increasing, is she?"

"No!" he protested with a laugh.

"Wellborn, then, although I have never heard mention of her name?"

After hesitating a moment, he answered, "She is related to Lady Polstead."

"That is not a recommendation, but I daresay she's held to be handsome."

"That is a matter of . . . opinion."

"Doubtless she comes with a large portion to her name."

"Nothing to speak of, Aunt."

All at once Lady Brimston sat up, swinging her legs over the edge of the daybed. "No fortune, no great beauty, and not even wellborn! Carisbrooke, I commend you. I fancy you must be head over tip in love with the girl!"

The marquess had the grace to look embarrassed, a rare occurrence to those who knew him. "I need your assistance, Aunt."

Once again, her eyes narrowed and she said, "Oh, yes . . . ?" as she reached out for a sugarplum to pop into her mouth.

"Arabella, my wife, is unused to the ways of the ton. I need someone to show her how to dress and conduct herself—not that she hasn't got pretty manners," he added

126

hastily as his aunt subjected him to a most discomforting stare.

"Not to mention, procure for her vouchers for Almack's."

Her nephew smiled. "That would be very much appreciated, Aunt."

"I really ought to refuse."

The marquess leaned forward. "There is no one else I can ask, at least no one who is so accomplished and has so many connections."

"You're pouring the butterboat over me. Well, I tell you, your moonshine cannot move me. I have been too ill-used."

"That is a great pity, Aunt Ernestine, for you have all the rank and connections, but if you won't help Lady Carisbrooke, I shall be obliged to ask Cousin Wolsingham."

"There, there, Carisbrooke, I didn't say I wouldn't help you with this creature," she answered, and he let out a faint sigh of relief. "In truth, you have me intrigued. There's more to this than you are willing to say, but for now I'll agree to assist your wife. Any female who is brave enough to marry you is deserving of every assistance she is able to receive. Fanny Wolsingham has no consequence at all, so you will forget about asking her."

"Naturally," he agreed, smiling with satisfaction.

"Now, apart from vouchers to Almack's, tell me exactly what it is you have in mind. . . ."

Chapter Fifteen

$\mathcal{B}$y the time Arabella had explored just a small part of her husband's Grosvenor Square house, she acknowledged the truth of his claim that it was the largest town house in London.

She had left the massive suite of rooms assigned to her on her arrival, and investigated countless bedchambers and salons before she came upon the ballroom. It was large enough to hold at least five hundred people, with great Venetian chandeliers hanging from the ceiling. It was here she was expected to preside over spectacular routs and soirees, a feat achieved by only the most experienced hostesses. How she could accomplish such a triumph so soon after being installed in the mansion she had no notion, for she couldn't even find her way to any of the drawing rooms.

Eventually she was obliged to swallow her pride and ask a footman, who inquired, "Which drawing room does your ladyship require?"

"Any," she answered in desperation. "A small one preferably."

No sooner had she been ushered into a pleasant room overlooking the extensive gardens at the rear of the house than another servant announced the arrival of a visitor. Arabella had only just opened her library book and surprise rendered her incapable of pleading indisposition, or indeed any other excuse, before an awesome lady swept into the room.

"I am Lady Brimston," she boomed, "your husband's aunt."

Overawed by the majestic sight of this influential lady, Arabella swept into a deep curtsy. "Yes, I know, my lady. My husband speaks of you fondly."

"Ha! He was correct in one particular: you do have pretty manners, and even if I detect a jot of insincerity, it is evident you mean well. Stand up straight and let me have a proper look at you."

For a few moments Arabella was obliged to endure the older woman's scrutiny. She tried not to flinch or blush, but could not be certain she did either.

"The Pain and Passion of Love!" her ladyship declared, and Arabella realized she was repeating the title of the book still clutched in her hands.

"I just . . . picked it up in a hurry. . . ."

"Rather good I thought when I read it." Arabella had no opportunity to savor even a modicum of relief before her husband's aunt went on, "Remove your spectacles this instant."

Arabella snatched them from her nose, explaining, "I have only just purchased them, having left my others behind. . . ."

"You must not in any circumstances allow yourself to be seen wearing them in company, and never, ever, in the society of your husband. Moreover, don't even hint that you might be a bluestocking, for that way lies social ruin."

"Yes, my lady," Arabella managed to stammer. "I assure you, I have no leanings toward intellectual pursuits."

"Well, I consider you tolerably fetching, whatever Carisbrooke says to the contrary."

Arabella looked horrified. "What *does* he say?"

But her husband's alarming aunt merely added, "The gown you're wearing is simply hideous."

Arabella bridled. "Your nephew ordered it for me when we were at Abbey Dulcis."

"From Annie McFee, no doubt. It bears her hallmark of dressmaking, at least two Seasons out of date and country-dowd style. It will have to go."

Before Arabella could protest that she had nothing else to wear, save what Mrs. McFee had made for her, the countess strode to the door and barked an order. In response, a stream of liveried servants marched in carrying numerous garments, which they laid with great reverence over the sofas and chairs before they withdrew. Others followed with stacks of boxes, which they placed carefully on the floor.

From their midst a lady emerged. She was small and exquisitely dressed, and she scrutinized Arabella as thoroughly as Lady Brimston had done minutes earlier.

"Well, what do you say, madame?" the countess demanded. "Does she have possibilities?"

"Lady Brimston!" Arabella protested.

"Definitely, my lady," the newcomer replied in a heavily accented voice. "Her ladyship is not all perfection, but with my assistance, she will soon be out of the ordinary, I assure you."

"What is going on here?" Arabella asked.

Ignoring her, the mantua-maker continued, "It is most fortunate that a very little alteration is all that is necessary to fit her ladyship into these gowns."

Lady Brimston smiled at last, and Arabella cried, "Will you both kindly cease to speak of me as if I were not here!" The other two ladies fell silent and stared at her in astonishment. "I beg your pardon, my lady," Arabella added, averting her eyes, "but could someone kindly explain *what all this is about*?"

"A stroke of good fortune, my dear. Madame LeFevre recently arrived from Paris with a huge consignment of fashions ordered by a city merchant's wife. However, the gentleman now finds himself financially embarrassed, and Madame LeFevre is in possession of what might have been useless merchandise."

"A few tucks and stitches is all that is necessary to make them fit, your ladyship," the mantua-maker declared, signaling to her assistant, "if the fashions please you."

Arabella had only managed a glimpse of what the gowns were like, but they did appear exquisite. *"If?"* she chuckled as the mantua-maker brandished her tape measure while her assistant began to unhook the offending gown.

Lady Brimston seated herself in a prominent position to watch Arabella trying on the succession of garments. After the similar stratagem employed by her husband, Arabella was less embarrassed by her presence than she might have been. Besides, she was fascinated by the vast array of garments brought before her, so many that soon her head began to spin.

There were day dresses in poplin, chintz, and Indian cottons, as well as the finest lawns and muslins, ball gowns in beautiful chiffons, sarcenets, and silks, beaded, spangled, and appliqued in the most ornate manner. Arabella gasped each time she looked in the mirror and saw herself transformed by clothes even finer than those worn by her cousin. Velvet and fine wool pelisses came complete with matching bonnets, reticules, and muffs. All the while Madame LeFevre's assistants were busily engaged in altering those garments she had tried on. A ready-made collection of clothes direct from Paris was more than she could have hoped for.

"My lady, I really don't know how to express my gratitude to you," Arabella sighed as she pirouetted in an

131

apricot gauze ball gown that would, with a few extra stitches, fit her like another skin.

"Now you do look more suited to be my nephew's wife."

"It is very kind of you to trouble on my behalf."

"It's no secret that Carisbrooke is a particular favorite of mine."

While Arabella was divested of the ball gown and helped into a muslin day gown with scalloped hem and puffed sleeves, she mused, "You must be curious about the suddenness of our marriage."

"Carisbrooke is at the same time both rational and impetuous, so nothing he is like to do astonishes me overmuch. His taste in females has always been on the flamboyant side, whereas you are a pleasant surprise and a considerable relief. I question no further than that."

"No one could possibly compare me to the beauties Lucian previously courted."

"Thank the Lord! Don't mistake me, my dear, you are quite a taking chit, and your figure is one to be envied. It is just that you are not handsome in a vulgar way, nor do you appear airheaded. I am satisfied with his choice."

Affected by these words, Arabella's eyes misted, and she turned to the countess. "Oh, my lady, how kind of you to say so."

Lady Brimston was subjecting Arabella to her feared gimlet stare. "Unless you can give me a reason not to rejoice."

Arabella was unable to look away until Madame LeFevre interrupted most welcomely to say, "This is the last gown, my lady. With your permission, I will take away those still to be altered and return with them on the morrow. In the meantime your ladyship will have sufficient choice from those already completed."

"I'm obliged to you," the new Lady Carisbrooke murmured as she allowed the gown to be peeled off her.

"Choose something to wear," Lady Brimston ordered. "Then we can go to Piccadilly and procure the rest of what is needed," a declaration that made Arabella laugh.

"I cannot conceive what is left for me to purchase!"

"Gloves, shifts, bed gowns, stockings, and so forth."

Arabella's head swam as she surveyed the array of clothes, fitted to her measurements. "I don't know which to put on. They're all so beautiful."

Emitting an exasperated sigh, the countess got to her feet and lumbered across the room. "If you continue to be so indecisive about your apparel, you're doomed to be late at every engagement, and that is something that will do nothing to sweeten your husband's disposition. The eau-de-nil poplin and the emerald green velvet pelisse is suitable for the purpose," she said shortly. "Now, don't hang in the hedge, my dear. There is much left to be done."

Arabella's newly appointed abigail quickly helped her dress and, feeling more than a little self-conscious in her fine new clothes, she allowed herself to be hurried out to the old-fashioned landau, standing in front of the house, by a lady who had evidently handed down her overweening ways to her nephew.

Chapter Sixteen

$\mathscr{B}$y the time she returned to Grosvenor Square several hours later, by way of a stop at Gunter's for ices, Arabella's head was still reeling. The extent of Lady Brimston's purchases on her behalf was on a scale of extravagance that outstripped even Lady Polstead. However, there was no gainsaying so determined a lady, and the items chosen were gleefully wrapped by obliging clerks working for the various haberdashers and mercers they visited. In fact, Arabella was quite convinced they had called at every warehouse in the capital.

The moment she entered the hall, accompanied by a small army of footmen, who were necessary to carry the parcels from Lady Brimston's carriage, she encountered the marquess, who was proceeding down the stairs. He paused halfway, and Arabella waited self-consciously in the middle of the hall while he thoroughly scrutinized her appearance. She was aware how well the green pelisse flattered her coloring and wearing a matching shako-style hat, adorned by a single silk tassel, she appeared as fashionable as anyone she was likely to encounter, but she still found the inspection profoundly disconcerting. The intensity of his stare caused her cheeks to flame, and she averted her eyes in the hope he wouldn't notice her discomposure.

"Very fetching," he commented at last, and then continued down the stairs. "It is evident Aunt Ernestine has called on you."

"She had the most tremendous good fortune in locating a consignment of ready-made clothes from Paris. Then her ladyship insisted we purchase a prodigious number of accessories to go with them. I'm persuaded, Lucian, it has all cost an absolute fortune."

"Judging by the dramatic transformation in your appearance, Belle, it's worth every penny piece."

Once again, her cheeks grew warm, but she couldn't help chuckling. "I'm not sure that's a compliment, Lucian."

"It's not like you to be so missish," he told her, extinguishing her brief pleasure in his approval. Then he put a light hand on her arm, and she had the vague suspicion he too was somewhat discomposed, although she couldn't comprehend why he should be. "I'm having your new racing curricle brought around. It's time we were seen out together. Curiosity about you is reaching fever pitch."

She started and shied away from his touch. "I'm not sure . . ."

"I am. When I sparred with Loudon at Gentleman Jackson's this morning, he told me he is engaged to ride with your cousin in the Park this afternoon. There couldn't be a better time for you to make your debut in Society."

She backed away from him even farther. "No, Lucian, I really can't face her just yet. Give me a little more time to grow used to my new circumstances."

He cast her a mocking look. "The encounter will be for only a fleeting moment. Come along, Belle, I never believed you to be so hen-hearted. You always seemed to possess copious amounts of pluck."

"I am not hen-hearted!" she protested. "I am merely breathless from the pace of events."

"That will be all to the good. You won't have any time to fret."

He led her down the steps just as the splendid new curricle, complete with aristocratic escutcheon and team of matching bay horses, was drawing up outside. At the sight of it Arabella's resistance melted.

"Oh, Lucian, it's beautiful, but far too grand for the likes of me."

"Stuff and nonsense, Belle. Recall you are now Lady Carisbrooke, not Arabella Trentham, and nothing but the best will do. Your new position conveys upon you a good deal of consequence. No one clapping eyes on you will associate you with the dowd from Polstead House."

He helped her onto the box, and as always, his proximity was deeply affecting. By the time he joined her, she was reasonably composed and told him, "I find it difficult to remember my new situation in life."

"You'll soon grow accustomed to it, especially when members of the ton begin to pay their respects, as they will, very shortly now. You'll probably be beseiged by toadeaters."

Arabella chuckled again, her good spirits returning. "Monk said much the same to me when we were at Abbey Dulcis, but I really cannot conceive of it."

He paused to gaze at her. "Aunt Ernestine has really achieved wonders. She's thrust you into the high crack of fashion."

She bridled, answering tartly, "It is not Lady Brimston who is wearing these clothes to advantage."

"You've already turned toplofty," he told her as he handed her the whip and the ribbons.

"If I have, you have only yourself to blame."

Once again, she shrank away from him, and he urged, "Come along, Belle, you know you are able to cut a dash with the best of them."

136

"But not in the Park! Not at the fashionable hour. I'm bound to make a cake of myself."

"There is no other time to go," he responded with what she considered to be maddening complacency.

She snatched the whip and took up the ribbons, more sharply than intended. Biting her lip with concentration, she set the team in motion and drove out into the square, trying not to be too conscious of the man sitting next to her with his arms folded in front of him, but failing completely.

"Your faith in me might be entirely misguided," she ventured as she carefully negotiated the traffic.

"Just knowing you are the Marchioness of Carisbrooke is sufficient to make your cousin as mad as a weaver. Why else was she at pains to keep you in reduced circumstances when she could have so easily assisted you in making a congenial marriage? She perceived you as a rival from the start."

In exasperation she cried, "I truly cannot comprehend why you're so intent upon pursuing this lunatic course!"

"You should," he answered as he leaned forward to correct a slight movement to the left. "Any other female would be only too glad to be turned into a lady, regardless of the reason, without the endless quizzing."

"I was always a lady. I simply have a title now, and much good it is doing me."

"Just glance in a looking glass, Belle, and you'll see what good it *has* done."

Arabella couldn't argue with him. The reflection she had gazed at in astonishment was far preferable to that dowdy creature who had lived anonymously in her cousin's house, but any degree of elevation was worthless if it failed to attain the affection of the man she loved.

"I paid a courtesy call on the Russian Ambassador this morning." He paused before adding, "I informed him we wished to hold a grand ball in honor of the czar at Carisbrooke House."

The shock resulting from his statement caused her to lose control of the team, and he hastily took hold of the ribbons as the carriage emerged into Park Lane.

"That is an awesome responsibility," she gasped as he handed back control of the curricle. "I'm not sure I am up to it."

"Don't worry your head about the fine details. I'll ask Lady Brimston to oversee the organization. All you need to do is choose your most fetching gown for the event."

For a few moments Arabella concentrated on driving the curricle through the gates of Hyde Park, aware that their arrival was causing heads to turn. It was not an unpleasant experience.

"Don't, I beg of you, trouble your aunt, Lucian. I shall do all that is necessary."

"Don't fly up into the boughs, Belle, but you must understand a diversion of this kind needs an expert hand."

"Tell me, Lucian, do you regard Lady Polstead as an accomplished hostess?"

She discerned that he drew a sharp breath. "It would be churlish of me to regard her as anything less."

"No one is supposed to know, but Kitty used to decide to have routs and soirees, then leave all the preparations for me to execute."

He sat forward on the box, gazing at her in astonishment while all those around them were exhibiting unashamed curiosity about Lord and Lady Carisbrooke. Gentlemen were raising their hats, ladies were gazing at them and talking excitedly between themselves, no doubt discussing the perceived virtues and deficiencies of the new marchioness.

"You're roasting me, Belle."

"I am not."

"No, indeed you are not." He sighed, sinking back again.

"If you had known about it, would you have admired her less? Would anyone? I think not. I engaged the caterers, florists, and musicians, and only consulted Kitty regarding the kind of food she wished to be served. Anything out of season, naturally, the most expensive commodities, needless to say. *And*," she added, "I made certain my cousin wasn't overcharged for a single item supplied to Polstead House!"

"I can believe it," he answered in a tone dripping with irony.

Arabella had been obliged to slow the curricle to a walking pace because of the large number of carriages, most of them slowing almost to a standstill to catch a glimpse of the new Marchioness of Carisbrooke.

The marquess raised his hat as a splendid barouche drew alongside. "Lady Hertford, do allow me to present my wife. This is her first public outing since our marriage."

"My lady, this is an honor," Arabella stammered, staring at the Prince Regent's latest paramour with great surprise, for the lady was scarcely a beauty and, as far as she could make out, on the shady side of forty.

"I'm delighted to make the acquaintance of the lady who has snared London's most eligible bachelor into the parson's mousetrap. We must take tea together, my dear, and you can tell me how you achieved such a remarkable feat."

"I'm most obliged to you, ma'am," Arabella replied with due reverence, "and I look forward to it with relish."

As they drove on, the marquess told her, "There'll be no problem procuring vouchers to Almack's now. You have charmed her ladyship with great ease."

"I believe it was you she responded to, and if she

139

invites me to take tea with her, I shall be obliged to divulge the true secret of how I snared the most eligible bachelor in the ton into the parson's pound."

He roared with laughter, setting her quaking with merriment too. Then a moment later Arabella's laughter faded when she spotted her cousin driving toward them in Lord Loudon's high-perch phaeton. Her husband also reverted to a more serious mood, moving closer to Arabella and slipping his arm along the back of her seat, giving the distinct impression he was possessive of his new wife. Arabella didn't know which made her more uncomfortable—the closeness of her husband or her cousin's stony countenance.

"By Jove! At last! Lady Carisbrooke," Lord Loudon cried. "What a picture. For once the tattle baskets don't exaggerate your loveliness. So divine. Lucky fellow, Carisbrooke!"

Lady Polstead inclined her head unsmilingly as the carriages passed with what seemed to be tortuous slowness. The marquess smiled roguishly at his former lover while raising his hat with perfect politeness.

"Your cousin doesn't appear overjoyed at your stroke of good fortune," he commented when the phaeton had passed.

"Lucian, it really isn't wise to make an enemy of her."

"It's too late to make dainty on that score. I confess, I am not quaking in my boots."

"That is because you're a fool," she snapped.

Ignoring her ill humor, he merely ordered, "Drive on, Belle. Princess Lieven is coming in this direction, and I would have you make acquaintance with her."

"I might have guessed Carisbrooke would only become leg-shackled to a beauty, even though you hinted

140

she was bracket-faced," Lord Loudon commented as he drove away.

"That is no beauty," his companion snapped, lowering her parasol and jabbing it in his direction. "She is my cousin, done up like one of Prinny's banquets."

"Well, I still maintain you have a handsome family, ma'am."

"Oh, do be silent, Loudon. You're giving me the headache with your endless prattling. If you can't find anything to say of greater significance, I beg you to desist."

"Beg pardon, ma'am," muttered the chastened gentleman.

"Did you see her hat?"

"Very fetching," he murmured with no apparent interest.

"It was so modish. Utterly divine, in fact. I'll wager they've just returned from Paris. Her clothes couldn't possibly have come from an English seamstress. It's past all bearing, Loudon. Why, she's nothing but a mushroom. How dare she have the effrontery to come back to London and disport herself in this manner?"

"Perhaps she's doing it just to vex you, my dear," Lord Loudon suggested helpfully.

"Oh, indeed, I'm persuaded that is precisely her reason, and I'm resolute she will not succeed!"

"Kitty, dearest," a lady called from the window of a passing barouche, "I have just clapped eyes upon Carisbrooke and his bride."

"It would be a trifle difficult not to see her in that vulgar equipage," Lady Polstead replied caustically.

"No one's in the least surprised she's a dasher, but you must feel satisfied that it was you who engineered such a brilliant match."

"Oh, take me out of here, Loudon!" her ladyship

141

entreated, sinking back into the satin cushions with one hand clasped to her head. "I cannot endure a moment longer!"

Chapter Seventeen

The very next morning, having brooded all night on the encounter in Hyde Park with Kitty, Arabella decided to call around at Polstead House in the hope of making her peace with her cousins—or at least negotiate an uneasy truce. She was aware Lucian would not approve of such a course, but she really couldn't bear to remain at daggers drawn with her own relatives when they were bound to enounter one another often from now on. Molly was another very important reason she didn't wish to stay on bad terms with Kitty. Arabella aspired to see the child as often as she could, and desperately hoped Kitty wouldn't be so angry she'd withhold that privilege.

Without Lucian's guiding hand, Arabella chose not to drive herself in the curricle and instead traveled the short distance to Polstead House in the Carisbrooke barouche. Her knees were decidedly shaky when she climbed down outside her cousin's mansion. She gazed up at the frontage for a few moments, attempting to compose herself and still the fluttering inside her. It seemed incredible that only a short time ago she set off from this very house to be propelled into a situation she could not have foreseen even in her most fanciful moments.

"Miss Trentham," the house steward greeted her, looking somewhat surprised. "I do beg your pardon, ma'am, for the oversight. It is Lady Carisbrooke now, is it not?" Still unused to that form of address, she looked away from the blatant curiosity in his eyes. "I'm sure Mrs. Perdy and all the other servants would want to join me in wishing you happy, my lady."

"Thank you, Kingsley. Your good wishes are very much appreciated. Is . . . is her ladyship at home?"

"Sir Andrew and Lady Polstead left for a short sojourn in Paris this very morning, my lady."

Arabella was both dismayed and relieved. "I don't suppose Miss Polstead has gone with them."

The ghost of a smile crossed the man's face. "Miss Polstead was sent to the country with Miss Byford some days ago, my lady."

As she walked slowly down the steps to the waiting carriage, Arabella reflected that she might have guessed Kitty would remove Molly from her sphere without even considering the consequences of such a step on the child.

She was still feeling considerably down pin when she arrived back at Grosvenor Square a short while later, only to encounter a stranger in conversation with the house steward in the hall. The moment she entered the house, the newcomer turned on his heel and she saw he was of a similar age to her husband; but whereas Lucian was as dark as Lucifer, this man was fair-haired with blue eyes that sparkled when they alighted on her.

"Lady Carisbrooke?" His voice was lightly accented. "Allow me to introduce myself." He took her hand and bowed over it. "Count Vladimir Gronski at your service."

"Did you wish to speak with my husband, Count?"

He let her hand go. "That was certainly my intention, but in his lordship's absence I am delighted to address myself to you." Arabella averted her eyes from his admiring look. "I arrived in London recently, accompanying the Archduchess Catherine. Her Excellency wishes

144

to express her appreciation for your proposed hospitality to her and her brother, the czar."

"It will be our pleasure, Count," she managed to reply, still unable to envisage herself hosting such a grand function.

The count was eyeing her in a manner she found distinctly discomfiting, one to which she was not accustomed. She was sure she could not be mistaken about the admiration in his manner toward her.

"In truth, my lady, I had not expected to find someone so young."

"Are you afraid I won't be able to host such an important diversion?"

The young man looked aghast. "By no means! It is just a pleasant surprise. Your husband is to be commended for his willingness to share so precious a treasure as you, my lady, with his guests." Arabella laughed delightedly as he added, "I was warned that English ladies resembled bears and were twice as ferocious, so you must forgive my prodigious surprise."

"Oh, Count!" she protested, "I can see I shall be obliged to educate you on that score!"

"If every other lady I encounter possesses just a little of your beauty and a grain of your wit, my lady, then I will consider my visit to this country a great success."

"But, surely, you haven't come just to admire English ladies."

"Not officially, of course. . . ."

They were laughing merrily when the marquess strode into the hall, tossing his hat and riding whip at the house steward at the same time as assessing the situation; his modish wife laughing companionably with the handsome stranger. There was something about their camaraderie that irked, although he couldn't comprehend why that should be.

145

Lord Carisbrooke eyed the count while he addressed Arabella. "It's good to see you so well diverted in my absence."

She quickly explained Count Gronski's purpose in calling, and as urbane as ever, but displaying a certain stiffness of bearing, he invited the Russian to join him in his study. As the two gentlemen moved across the hall, the marquess hesitated to survey his wife, who was wearing another of Madame LeFevre's fine creations. It startled him to observe how easily she had become the stunning creature he required of her, and he wondered why he wasn't more delighted at the transformation. In truth, he was startled at how little it had taken to effect the change in her; a new wardrobe of clothes, a few lessons in driving and dancing to polish her abilities, and the deed was done. The little moth needed only the slightest encouragement to emerge as a brilliant butterfly.

"I very much hope we will meet again soon, my lady," Count Gronski told her, taking her hand once more.

"I'm sure we shall, Count," Arabella responded coolly, unnerved by her husband's overbearing presence.

The easy rapport she'd enjoyed with the count seemed no longer attainable when observed by the marquess.

He too made a stiff little bow. "By your leave, my dear."

When they had gone, she drew a faint sigh, having decided it was far preferable to be esteemed rather than overlooked as she had been for the first three and twenty years of her life, but it would be better still if the admirer was Lucian, Marquess of Carisbrooke.

"I hear that Kitty Polstead has just returned to town from Paris, in possession of an entire new wardrobe of clothes," Lady Brimston commented as she and Arabella drove back to Grosvenor Square. She chuckled. "I don't suppose anyone should wonder why she considered it necessary to make the journey."

"My cousin is always exquisite whatever she wears," Arabella answered in a muted tone.

"She also knows full well how to wheedle her own way with gullible gentlemen. I'm more than grateful to you, my dear, for rescuing my crack-brained nephew from her clutches."

Arabella smiled wanly and stared down at her mittened hands. "Lucian rendered me a similar service. I find my new situation far more preferable to the one I held before my marriage."

"Lady Polstead certainly succeeded in keeping you least in sight, for I don't recall ever clapping eyes on you in her house, but it is evident Carisbrooke was more fortunate in doing so."

Arabella didn't gainsay the countess, who had been very kind to her since her return to London and had been instrumental in fixing her place in Society. As Lucian's wife, there was no question of not being accepted into the beau monde, but being taken up by no less a personage than Lady Brimston smoothed her way considerably. Everyone, Arabella noted, was anxious to please the countess, who still remained formidable but no longer appeared so fearsome.

"By the by," her ladyship confided as the barouche entered the carriage drive of Carisbrooke House, "my son has returned to town. He called upon me this morning."

Arabella's smile was genuine now. "I'm so glad, my lady. It will be good to see him again."

Lady Brimston cast her a wry look. "He declares himself eager to renew his acquaintance with you."

Arabella was still smiling when she entered the magnificent portals of Carisbrooke House. It was now usual to find countless invitations to forthcoming functions awaiting her whenever she arrived home. Although she read all of them with interest, she was still obliged to leave Lucian to decide which of them to accept, although she had an inkling which was *bon ton* and which was not from addressing her cousin's invitations and acknowledgment cards.

Kitty. Now she was back from Paris, Arabella acknowledged they were bound to attend many of the same functions. Although it was inevitable they would come face-to-face again very soon, that was something Arabella didn't relish. It was not out of fear of any unpleasantness that might ensue, but because she hated the false role she was forced to play. However much she might try to deny it to herself, she was resentful of the hold that woman still retained on the heart of her husband.

No sooner had Arabella discarded her bonnet and pelisse than the house steward announced the arrival of none other than Lady Polstead herself. For a moment or two Arabella was paralyzed with fear, but then she recovered herself sufficiently to order her cousin shown into the sunny little drawing room she had chosen as her personal domain.

By the time her cousin swept into the room, Arabella was outwardly composed, standing by the window, her hands clasped in front of her. From the uncompromising expression on Kitty's face, it was immediately evident she had not come to wish Arabella well in her marriage. She did, however, look wonderful. Undoubtedly her appearance was enhanced by her new Parisian rig out.

"Kitty," Arabella greeted her, forcing a smile of welcome to her face. "How lovely to see you. I did call in on you several days ago to pay my respects."

Her cousin glanced around the room, taking in the opulence of the furnishings and the little telltale signs that showed Arabella had made it her own. "So I was informed."

"I was disappointed not to see Molly."

Kitty returned her attention to her cousin. "Molly has gone down to Thirlmere for the duration."

Arabella made a great effort to hide her disappointment behind a bright smile. "I shall miss her, Kitty. Will she be returning to town in the near future?"

"No. A period of rustication was thought advisable because she was utterly heartbroken at your defection and could not be consoled."

The new Lady Carisbrooke twisted her hands in anguish. "I'm truly sorry to hear you say so, but perhaps you would allow me to try to make amends by taking her out and spending time with her as I was used to do."

"That would not be desirable. Molly wouldn't want it."

Arabella emitted a little sigh of dismay before inviting, "Do stay and take tea with me."

As Arabella went to pull the bell cord, her cousin snapped, "Despite your attempts to give yourself airs, I don't intend to mince words with you a moment longer. This was not intended to be a social call. I merely wished to tell you how disappointed I am with you."

Abandoning all hopes of appeasing her cousin and contriving to maintain her calm, Arabella replied. "That does not surprise me in the least. An elevated marriage was never your plan for me, and yet that is what I have managed to achieve."

Her cousin's eyes narrowed dangerously. "Just what do you think you're about, you scheming little minx?"

"Let's not quarrel, Kitty," Arabella begged. "I am sure you've already realized, I was compromised during my attempt to assist you, and Carisbrooke did the honorable thing by marrying me."

Lady Polstead's lip curled into the semblance of a smile. "At least you're not claiming he's madly in love with you, which would be the height of humdudgeon."

"The circumstances of my marriage are no longer important. I just wanted to make matters right with you in the hope we can remain friends."

"Those who are considered friends do not behave in such an underhanded way. Your disloyalty to me can never be forgiven. As you may know, Polstead has cast you out completely, and although we are bound to encounter one another at various diversions in the future, I take leave to inform you our relationship can never be mended."

Kitty Polstead turned on her heel, and as she rushed to the door, Arabella told her, "I cannot be sorry our relationship will never be as it was. If I hadn't married so far above me, I'd still be installed in your house as an unpaid servant."

Once again, Lady Polstead turned to face her cousin, her eyes narrowed angrily. "How dare you say so! I took you in when you had nowhere else to go!"

"No, you did not, Kitty. It was Andrew who took me in, and if I have angered him, then I am more sorry than I can say. I hope to be able to explain myself to him before long."

"Don't trouble yourself. You will find he won't listen to you. You can no longer grease his boots to good effect, for he sees you as the slyboots you undoubtedly are, and I have no doubt Lady Brimston will soon reach that conclusion too."

"Kitty, I beg of you, don't punish Molly in your anger toward me."

"You will never, ever again have access to my daughter," Lady Polstead vowed as she flounced out of the room, leaving her cousin wringing her hands in anguish and roundly blaming the whole sorry business on Lucian.

Chapter Eighteen

$\mathcal{A}$rabella was still shaking from her encounter with her cousin when Count Gronski was shown into the drawing room, and she made a great effort to greet him as effusively as his station decreed. His delight in finding her at home was, to some degree, a balm to her bruised emotions.

"Lady Carisbrooke, it is a personal pleasure for me to deliver felicitations to you and his lordship from the Archduchess Catherine. Finding you at home is a particular joy I did not look to see."

She took the note with an unsteady hand. "This is so kind of Her Excellency. I'm persuaded my husband will be equally pleased at her condescension."

"We are looking forward to the splendid diversions put on for the peace celebrations."

"We have all waited a long time for the opportunity to rejoice in Boney's downfall. Count Gronski, may I offer you some refreshment?"

"I do not wish to keep you, as I am sure your company must be much in demand."

She looked wry. "As it so happens, Count, it is not at this particular moment."

"If you were my wife," he declared with a fervor that took her aback, "I would not allow you out of my sight for one second. There are too many gentlemen minded to

152

dance attendance upon a lady as fetching as you."
Because she was unaccustomed to having the butterboat
poured over her in so blatant a manner, she blushed.
Before she could think of something suitable to say in
return, he continued, "Perhaps you would do me the very
great honor of accompanying me to Hyde Park, where
preparations are afoot for the victory celebrations. You
might find it diverting."

Because she felt more at ease with this charming
stranger than her own husband, she was just about to
accept when the marquess answered for her.

"I was about to make the same suggestion to my wife."

Arabella looked past the count to see the marquess
standing in the doorway. Count Gronski immediately
started to withdraw. "Another time perhaps, my lady."

"Certainly," she replied, casting Lucian a cold look.

When the courtier had bowed himself out of the room,
Lucian remarked, "He is becoming a barnacle. I don't
suppose I need ask why he was here."

Miffed by his overweening conduct, she informed
him, "He came to deliver a note from the Archduchess
Catherine."

She thrust it at him, and his eyebrows rose a little. "A
personal letter, eh? That is quite a coup."

"If you are envisaging Lady Polstead's reaction to all
this, I may as well tell you now, she called in just before
Count Gronski arrived."

"No wonder you appear blue-deviled."

"You'll be gratified to know, she was in something of a
miff and in no mood for reconciliation with her wicked
cousin."

He appeared unmoved by her heartfelt declaration.
"No doubt, you attempted to humor her."

"Naturally. I dislike being on the outs with anyone."

"You must resign yourself to the situation," he

advised, continuing to exhibit no real concern on the matter.

"Yes," she agreed with a sigh, "I'm persuaded I must."

He surveyed her with a disturbing intensity before he ordered, "Go upstairs and change, Belle. I'll have the horses brought 'round."

The use of her name, so softly on his lips, never failed to affect her, and her eyes began to mist with tears. Arabella quickly brushed past him and fled from the room.

When she came down a short while later, the horses were waiting outside in the care of their grooms. The marquess was booted and spurred, and when he took up his riding whip, he inspected her carefully. He displayed only the superficial interest in her she had become accustomed to enduring, but it still affected her deeply. It was much easier before he'd been aware of her existence, when she could feast her eyes on him as much as she wished without him being sensible of her presence.

"You have settled into your position admirably," he told her as they left the house.

Ironically his praise irked. "Naturally. You didn't marry a dishclout you rescued from the streets."

He eyed her wryly, commenting, "I wonder who put up your bristles? I rather fancy it was your cousin, but it could have been me, I suppose."

"Why do you say that?" she asked as he swung himself into the saddle.

He shrugged infinitesimally. "It occurs to me you wanted to go with Count Gronski to the Park, only my arrival ruined the opportunity."

"I'm sure there will be many more chances to ride with the count."

"He does have the look of a carpet-monger."

Arabella's eyes blazed angrily. "I resent the inference, Lucian."

154

"Oh, no insult intended, my dear," he answered easily, and before she could take the matter further, he asked, gazing ahead, his eyes firmly on the distance, "What did your cousin want?"

"Exactly what you might expect," she answered testily. "To inform me of her anger and disappointment. I'm not quite certain whether that is because I am married to you, or because she's lost a maid of all work. What do you think, Lucian?"

He turned in the saddle to smile at her. "I think it's simply because you have taken. You have, you know."

"Lady Brimston has been instrumental in any small success I might have achieved."

"You're being unnecessarily modest. You probably don't realize that you've become the most desirable woman in London."

Arabella reigned in her horse, causing the mare to snort with annoyance. Desirable to whom? she asked herself. Not to the one man in the entire world to whom she wanted to be alluring. It was all a horrible sham, and she couldn't bear it a moment longer. She dug in her heels and galloped away from him, heedless of where she was going. She just let her horse have its head until she saw the barriers ahead, and she was forced to pull on the reins once again. When the mare came to a shuddering halt, she slid out of the saddle, convulsed by silent sobs. Almost immediately Lucian rode up beside her, jumping to the ground at her side.

Beyond the barrier a full regiment of hussars was drilling with gun carriages in preparation for a twenty-one gun salute. The Prince Regent was also watching the proceedings from his high-perch phaeton, accompanied by several of his cronies and Lady Hertford.

The marquess turned her around to face him, asking, "What in tarnation is wrong with you, Belle?"

155

She wished she could tell him she loved him and had done so for months, from the very first moment she'd seen him walk into Polstead House to take Kitty riding. Instead she responded to his concerned touch by laying her cheek against his shoulder reveling in the way he kept his arm around her, holding her close while her tears flowed unchecked.

Why she was weeping even Arabella didn't know. Whether it was a reaction to Kitty's disturbing call, Molly's removal from London, or her own hopeless love, did not really matter just then. She could savor his closeness, luxuriate in the brief comfort he offered, and enjoy the feel of his hard body against hers.

A few moments later he held her at arm's length, scrutinizing her face and then, taking out his handkerchief, gently dabbing at her cheeks.

"Is this all a little too much for you?" he asked with a tenderness that almost set her weeping again. "Have I asked more of you than you're capable of giving?"

"No indeed," she sniffed, pride coming to the fore. "I'm being a goosecap. I'm overset by the way Kitty has spirited her daughter away to Thirlmere, mainly, I suspect, out of spite so I cannot see her."

Lucian looked at her keenly, still holding on to her, but she couldn't at that moment meet his eyes. "Nothing your cousin does should surprise you, Belle. Take comfort in the knowledge she cannot keep you apart forever."

"I'm afraid she can."

"I'm truly sorry," he told her, and she didn't doubt the sincerity of his words.

"She's a terribly lonely child, so it's Molly you should reserve your pity for. I don't care so much for myself, although, I confess, I do miss her a great deal."

When he drew her closer again, she didn't resist.

"Here, let me wipe the marks off your face. It wouldn't do if I was thought to be cruel to you so early in our marriage."

She laughed weakly as he dabbed at her face again. "No doubt if we'd been married longer, it would be quite acceptable."

"Naturally."

She was still laughing shakily when she looked up at him, and all at once her heart was beating wildly against her ribs. The way he was gazing back at her was something new and exciting.

"Belle," he whispered, drawing her against him.

Warmth surged through every fiber of her body as she waited breathlessly for his lips to meet hers. They seemed to hover over hers for a lifetime. His hand burned through the stuff of her pelisse and into her back. Longing coursed through her body, and she knew he couldn't fail to be aware of it. Just at that moment she was sure he felt it too in equal measure.

Then a discreet cough caused him to draw back. Arabella was left feeling desolate, never to know what might have happened next.

When they looked around, it was to see Lady Polstead accompanied by Lord Loudon and another half dozen of her cronies a few feet away. Kitty's expression was stony, but the others appeared amused, whether by what appeared to be a loving couple about to kiss or because of Lady Polstead's wrath, could not be ascertained.

"My wife appears to have a speck of dust in her eye," the marquess explained cheerfully, fully aware their intimacy would be interpreted otherwise by any onlooker.

One of the gentlemen laughed, and with a curt nod of her head, Kitty Polstead walked on, twirling her parasol as she went. When Lucian looked at Arabella again, she moved back to her horse, knowing with devastating certainty the moment was gone. It would probably never come again.

Chapter Nineteen

London was soon in the grip of frenzied activity with the arrival of the Czar of Russia and King Frederick William of Prussia, and their respective entourages. With so much to divert her attention, Arabella had no opportunity to grieve for her empty marriage. In no time at all she had been caught up in a giddy whirl all over town. The newly wed couple was in great demand for all the most fashionable functions. It couldn't have been better for the marquess's plan. Arabella was feted wherever she went, although he had known from the outset his wife was bound to be taken up. Arabella wondered if any of those courting her so assiduously recalled the dowdy creature who invariably seated herself at the back of the room and was generally ignored by everyone.

The new Lady Carisbrooke was considered to be handsome yet lacking in the overbearing sense of consequence so often found in those suddenly elevated to a high position, thus finding favor with the influential matrons of the ton. Only Sir Andrew and Lady Polstead cut her whenever their paths happened to cross, but as it was invariably in large establishments where they could stay in separate rooms, it was not noticeable to others and only aroused a faint sadness in Arabella. Had circumstances been different, she and Kitty could have cut a great dash together.

Fortunately, she had managed to make contact with Molly, who replied to a tentative letter by sending a hand-stitched sampler that Arabella framed and hung in her boudoir.

Invitations to the ball in honor of the Allies had been dispatched, written in her own copperplate hand, so prized by her cousin. The Carisbrookes had received no invitations from the Polsteads, so Arabella had no way of knowing who was writing theirs now. She was fully aware of the irony of the situation; the more successfully she played her role, the sooner she would be consigned to that lonely villa in Hans Town or Hampstead, leaving her husband free to seek the company of females more to his taste.

Whenever she wasn't being paraded around the town by the marquess, Arabella had Lady Brimston as a companion, or Count Gronski as an escort as well as Henry Brimston. When she was with Lucian, he acted so proud of her, she could almost believe it was true, and if she allowed thoughts of reality to invade her mind too often, her heart might break.

After the arrival of the czar, the Carisbrookes, Lady Brimston, and her son were driven to Piccadilly to see him appear on the balcony of Pulteney's Hotel. Count Gronski emerged onto the balcony too with the Archduchess Catherine of Oldenburg, and as the Carisbrooke party cheered along with everyone else, the count singled Arabella out for a cheery wave of his hand.

"You appear to have found an admirer," Lucian said in a voice dripping with irony.

"Not the only one, I trust," his aunt snapped in the manner that at one time would have intimidated Arabella.

In the silence that ensued, Lord Brimston put in, "Anyone acquainted with Lady Carisbrooke is bound to admire her."

"I'm obliged to you, Monk," Arabella responded, glancing sideways at Lucian. "One would almost believe my husband is jealous of the count."

"Most unnatural if he wasn't resentful of anyone dancing attendance on you, my dear," Henry Brimston answered with a gruff laugh.

The marquess smiled engimatically. "It's true my wife has become one of the most sought-after females in town since our marriage."

As she twirled her parasol, Arabella replied, "That is absolutely correct, dearest, and for it I am most indebted to you."

"Arabella," he started in a tone that denoted his irritation at her satisfied smile. Not only did his manner indicate her words had irked him, but he rarely called her Arabella nowadays.

As the royal party went inside the hotel at last and the crowd began to disperse, Lady Brimston mused, possibly in an attempt to forestall the quarrel brewing between her volatile niece and nephew, "Prinny seems to be playing least in sight, which is strange as he has orchestrated all these wonderful celebrations."

"It's because of Princess Caroline," her son explained. "She is determined to be a part of it, and Prinny cannot prevent her popping up everywhere, to his great embarrassment."

"Abandoned wives have a right to feel aggrieved," Arabella declared, casting her husband a challenging look.

"So you are a supporter of the princess," Lucian ventured, looking at her with interest.

"I believe, along with many others, she has been treated unfairly by her husband."

"You'd better make sure you behave correctly to Lady C.," Monk broke in, "or her fury will know no bounds. Not that it's in the least conceivable that you would ever wish to forsake her ladyship," he added hastily.

"This conversation is growing too tedious to be endured a moment longer," the marquess replied, sounding bored.

"You can be certain of one thing," Lady Brimston interjected, "there are a score of men ready and willing to jump into your shoes, Carisbrooke, should you be foolish enough to neglect your wife. Let's go to the Park," she suggested. "We might just catch sight of those ferocious Cossacks who came over with the czar."

"I clapped eyes on them for the very first time the other day while I was with Count Gronski," Arabella declared, her manner softening. "They actually carry spears!"

"Then, let us be away and see these amazing creatures," Lucian urged, and Arabella gained the distinct impression he was anxious to distance himself from Pulteney's Hotel.

A little farther away Lady Polstead was sitting in her landau, accompanied by several of her cronies, fully aware that the marquess and her cousin were in a carriage nearby.

"The Carisbrookes are to be special guests of the Archduchess Catherine at her reception," Mrs. Torrington-Gower informed her friend. "*And,* I am reliably informed, Lady Carisbrooke danced with the czar himself at Almack's."

"Oh, do hush," Lady Polstead replied, feigning boredom. "I don't care a brass button if they dined with the king at Windsor. Does no one ever talk of anyone else nowadays?"

Her friend looked crestfallen. "I thought you would care to know. After all, he acted the spoon over you."

"That only indicates what a clunch he must be."

"Do you hope to attend the ball at Carisbrooke House?"

Lady Polstead continued to feign a fashionable boredom. "Naturally. If I don't, there'll be any number of my acquaintances insisting on divulging every last trivial detail of it, so I may as well go myself."

"She is your cousin."

"That is my great misfortune."

Her friend smiled slyly. "You're just miffed because Carisbrooke no longer greases your boots."

"I'd already tired of his attentions," her ladyship assured her, "and it won't be long before that insipid creature bores him to death. Rely upon it, Hermione. When the *on dits* tell of a rift between them, remember I forecast it first. Drive on," she snapped at the coachman, "and let us resolve to talk of other things. Lady Carisbrooke is not the most interesting person in town at the moment."

"There are those who consider she is. Not only is she married to the divine marquess, but enjoys Count Gronski as an admirer too."

Lady Polstead sank back into the squabs, her eyes narrowed thoughtfully. "Yes, so she does," she murmured. "So she does."

The celebrations taking place in London's public and royal parks were in full swing. Persons of high and low birth mingled happily to rejoice at the end of the long war against Napoleon. The paths were crowded with riders on splendid horses. Those in military uniforms added color and even greater grandeur to the proceedings. Most people walked on the paths and grassy knolls. Even those who possessed carriages or horses found it more convenient to do so. So frenetic was all the activity that there arose a severe milk shortage because the large herds of cows that usually grazed peacefully in the parks had been frightened by the influx of humanity.

Arm in arm with her husband, Arabella wandered around the booths, marveled at the freak shows and jugglers, ate Regency cakes and sugarplums, laughed unreservedly at the antics of the Merry-Andrews, wondered at the balloon ascent, and considered she had never been so happy in her life.

In the ranks of the beau monde, there were a great many marriages contracted for reasons unconnected to love. If she didn't dwell too often on the inauspicious beginnings of their relationship, she could almost believe they were happily married, and she would have given anything to remain with him, even though her unspoken affection was not and never would be returned. But Arabella knew even this must soon end. Lucian would soon tire of attending her so assiduously, and the novelty of annoying Kitty was bound to lose its attraction before long. She didn't dare contemplate her fate when that occurred.

As they watched the mock naval battle on the *Serpentine*, Arabella wished Molly could have been in London to enjoy the spectacle too. Later that evening the celebrations reached a climax with a firework display at the end of which the Castle of Dismay was replaced miraculously by the Temple of Concord. Arabella took delight in everything she saw. It was a fantastic experience enhanced by the company of a man who was behaving in a particularly convivial manner.

From the midst of her adoring companions, Kitty Polstead was not so entranced by the spectacle. Her attention was attracted elsewhere. While Arabella was unaware of being closely observed, Lady Polstead eyed her cousin with no pleasure at all. Clad in her Parisian finery, Arabella glowed with youth, health, and happiness, and to any observer she and the marquess appeared to be a congenial pair, something remarked upon time and time again to Lady Polstead's fury.

When she spied Count Gronski coming in her direction, she detached herself from the group she was with and smiled enticingly at the Russian.

"Count Gronski," she greeted him, bestowing on him every vestige of charm she could muster. "I certainly didn't look to see you among the crowd this evening."

"The Grand Duchess and His Excellency are being entertained very well. I thought I might mingle a little. It is all so stupendous, I would like to experience some of the excitement felt by the ordinary citizens of this incredible city."

"Ah, such passion, Count. Could anyone express their feelings better than a Russian?" She slipped her arm into his. "Come, walk me back to my carriage," she invited. When he hesitated, she added slyly, "I'm persuaded the Archduchess will not miss you for a few more minutes. Perhaps you were seeking out one very special face in the crowd—not mine."

The young man became flustered as she led him away from Arabella and the marquess. "Indeed not, my lady. How can I be anything other than delighted to have encountered so gracious a lady?"

"You are gallant to say so, but I happen to be aware of your very great regard for my dear cousin."

"Then, I have been too obvious in my admiration. I have no wish to embarrass her."

"That is impossible. Moreover, I know full well that Lady Carisbrooke appreciates your regard, Count."

"Her ladyship is fortunate in having an adoring husband, which is no one's loss but my own."

"Appearances can be deceptive. Naturally, they *seem*

to have an accord, but I can assure you the truth is quite different. Lady Carisbrooke has a very high regard for propriety. That is both true and admirable, but she is also human. *Entre nous,* my dear count, I tell you the marriage is not, by any means, a love match." He looked startled. "It was contracted for dynastic purposes."

"They appear so well suited."

"Indeed, but their hearts are not engaged, which is of the greatest import in any relationship of worth, as you will no doubt agree. Unfortunately, the situation my cousin finds herself in is not unusual in my country or yours. I'm sure many such marriages are contracted in St. Petersburg."

"Mais, naturellement."

"In truth, since my cousin became acquainted with you, she has come to understand how empty her life has been—and will be again once you have returned to St. Petersburg. It is something she dreads wholeheartedly."

"I had no notion, my lady."

"How could you? My cousin would not speak of her misery, or, indeed, her feelings for you, but I am under no such constraint. Her future happiness means a great deal to me, and I know since you came to town, your company has made her more content than she has been since her marriage. When she appears to be radiant, I believe it is thoughts of you which renders her so."

"What you say to me gladdens my heart, my lady, and gives me much hope."

They had reached her carriage, and she turned to him to say in imploring tones, "Before you came, I despaired for her unhappiness, and my fear is for her sanity once you have gone."

"You need no longer harbor concerns on that score, my lady. Now you have made me sensible of the circumstances, I have no compunction in making my feelings

166

clear to her. I cannot leave her to wallow in suffering when true happiness is so close at hand."

"This is just the reaction I had hoped to glean from you, Count. You have not disappointed me, nor will you fail Lady Carisbrooke in her time of need." As he handed her into the carriage, she added, "My cousin possesses a very great sense of duty, Count. It might take a little effort for you to persuade her the true way of fulfillment, so I beg of you, do not give up if she resists you at first. I do so want to see her content at last."

"Nothing is closer to my heart," he assured her as he raised her hand to his lips. "I am indebted to you, my lady."

She ordered the coachman to drive on, and when she sank back into the squabs, her smile was one of profound satisfaction.

Chapter Twenty

"*T*here, my lady, you look an absolute treat," Arabella's maid declared, standing back to admire her mistress's appearance. "Doesn't she, Mrs. Turner?"

"That she does," the housekeeper answered, nodding her head with satisfaction.

The abigail was an experienced lady's maid, appointed by Lucian when they first arrived in London. It had been she who always ensured her mistress was turned out immaculately, and this particular evening was no exception. She had dressed Arabella's hair in a preponderance of curls, pinned into place by gold fillets. The apricot chiffon gown complemented her coloring, making her complexion appear translucent and her eyes seem a deeper green.

Even knowing she looked as fine as possible, Arabella was more nervous than ever, aware of the importance of the evening's events. She and Lucian were to host a function to which the czar, the King of Prussia, the Prussian princes, and the Regent himself were to attend. If it became the success Lucian hoped, the ball was likely to be talked about for years to come, and Arabella wanted fervently for it to be regarded as a great triumph for both their sakes.

An extravagant basket of flowers that had been sent by Count Gronski stood in one corner of the room, and the perfume emanating from it filled the air. On receiving it, Arabella tried to imagine how she would have felt if the card had borne her husband's name, but she was flattered by the count's attentions, which had grown more persistent in recent days. His regard was genuine. He sought her company because he wished to be with her, unlike her husband, who only attended her in public for his own dark reasons.

A brief knock at the door heralded his arrival, and she thought he had never looked more handsome. Her heart ached for something she had never known, nor ever would. She closed her eyes, imagining that he strode across the floor, crushed her in his arms, and kissed her until she was breathless.

Instead he said, "So you're dressed," as the two servants vacated the room. "You look very splendid," he added, but the compliment didn't seem to come from the heart and did nothing to gladden hers. "I brought you a little adornment," he went on, placing a large velvet box on a table.

"The Carisbrooke emeralds," she gasped when she saw the exquisite necklace with its matching bracelet and earrings.

"They could have been made for you," he told her as he placed the necklace around her throat and fastened it in position.

The combination of his touch on her neck and his breath on her cheek, induced her to become inordinately hot, despite the coolness of the gems against her skin. She fingered them self-consciously as he stepped back to admire the effect.

"Perfect," he declared.

Unable to control her bitterness a moment longer, she retorted, "For what purpose, pray? To adorn me? Or to vex my cousin who possesses countless jewels, but none quite as splendid as these?"

He remained irritatingly cool in the face of her anger. "Your nerves are understandably overset, and that is putting you out of humor."

"Pretense has cast me into the mopes."

All at once he caught sight of the flowers, and although there was no telling expression on his face, it was evident he was less than pleased when he said, "I see that Count Gronski has been overly attentive again. Such a generous gesture appears rather more significant than a simple token of appreciation."

"He's been very kind to me of late."

"You can attribute that particular skill to his expertise in greasing boots."

"Are you suggesting the count is insincere?"

"I am merely implying that to be a courtier to the czar, one needs to be a prize toadeater."

His scornful appraisal of the count imbued her with greater indignation. "That is a most ungracious thing to say about anyone, Lucian, let alone a gentleman who has been congenial to us both."

"It is nevertheless true," he replied, taking out an enameled snuffbox and extracting a pinch.

She eyed him resentfully as he closed the lid. "It was intended from the outset that I attract admiration from as many people as were willing to bestow it upon me."

He smiled without mirth as he replaced the snuffbox in the pocket of his dark blue evening coat. "You have succeeded beyond all my expectations, Belle."

She forced herself to face him squarely, and after taking a deep breath, demanded to know, "How long do you wish me to continue this masquerade? When will you concede my cousin has been sufficiently punished?"

His shoulders lifted into the slightest shrug. "Ongoing

torment is perhaps the best revenge of all. You appear to be enjoying all the attention you're receiving. You might as well continue—unless, of course, you have any other plans in mind."

When she made no reply, he snatched up her gossamer silk shawl and draped it around her unrelenting shoulders. He didn't immediately relinquish his hold on her, and she closed her eyes, the better to enjoy the feel of his hands on her shoulders. Once again, she was aware of the touch of his breath on her cheek. His lips were near to her face, so close it was well-nigh unbearable. The desire to turn and throw herself into his arms and declare her love for him was almost overwhelming.

Then he released his grip on her, and keeping her face averted lest he should detect her feelings, she went to take her reticule from the bed. From that moment onward there was little opportunity for Arabella to worry about the state of her emotions or the outcome of the ball. Once the first guests began to arrive, she took up her place at the head of the sweeping flight of stairs with her husband at her side. The ideal couple in the eyes of their acquaintance.

She greeted their royal guests with a curtsy and all others with as much charm as she could muster, aware all the while that Lucian was casting her sidelong glances. She felt no qualms, for she was sure she was playing her role to the hilt.

It was strange, almost dreamlike, finding herself hosting such a prestigious diversion, for she had often witnessed her cousin in this position, and never once had she wished to be in her place. When the Polsteads arrived, Arabella became tense again, and although Sir Andrew was rather brusque in his greeting, Kitty surprised her by smiling and behaving in a warmer manner than of late, which puzzled her cousin.

"Kitty seems to be accepting the situation at last,"

she whispered to Lucian after they had gone into the ballroom.

"Don't you know her better than that?" he replied before turning his considerable charm on the Duke of Clarence, who had just arrived.

As soon as the first dance was announced, Lucian partnered the Archduchess Catherine, and Arabella led the set with her brother, the czar. She experienced some misgivings when she observed Count Gronski partnering Kitty, but later when the count claimed Arabella for a stately minuet, she became bashful.

"Please accept my gratitude for the lavish gift of flowers."

"Nothing could be too extravagant for you, my lady. I hope you understand it signifies my great regard for you."

Arabella cast him an uneasy smile and was relieved when the dance began. Had Count Gronski attempted to court her while she had lived at Polstead House she would have been deliriously happy, but sadly she was aware he wouldn't have noticed Arabella Trentham any more than Lucian had.

Just when supper was announced and the majority of the guests swept out of the ballroom, Lady Polstead stayed behind and approached her cousin, whose heart thudded noisily and her palms grew moist, but she summoned a smile to her face and didn't wait until Kitty spoke first.

"I trust you're enjoying our little diversion."

"It's the best we've attended for an age." While Arabella was recovering from her surprise, Kitty went on. "Bella, the situation between us is so foolish. I confess the fault is in me, but you will perhaps understand and forgive the great shock your elopement caused."

"To me too," Arabella answered with a shaky laugh.

"Good. That is settled, then." She placed one hand over Arabella's. "The acrimony of the last few weeks must be consigned to the past." Count Gronski appeared at their side, and Lady Polstead cast him a conspiratorial smile. "I shall leave you to your other guests for now, but we will have a private coze very soon."

Her own escort was waiting patiently by the door, and she swept out leaving her cousin dumbstruck. Only when Count Gronski broke into her thoughts, saying, "Allow me to escort you into supper, my lady," did she recall he was there at all.

A little while later two guests were observing Lady Carisbrooke as she allowed the count to bring out her natural flirtatiousness.

"It's so odd no one knew of her before," one lady commented.

"They say she is related to Kitty Polstead," the other replied.

"That would account for her dazzling looks and explains how Carisbrooke became acquainted with her, for she did not come out."

"Lady Polstead might be a beauty, but she must be on the shady side of thirty. Lady Carisbrooke has her youth as an ally."

The marquess was standing nearby with some of his guests, but he too had been observing his wife with her admirer, her vivacity, the green sparkle in her eyes that dulled even the emeralds at her throat. As she responded with laughter to everything the count was saying to her, resentment bubbled up inside him. However, on hearing the two matrons, who were unaware of his proximity, he stepped forward to tell them, "It is true my wife has all of Lady Polstead's beauty and more, but she possesses nothing whatsoever of her character."

Later while Arabella paused to catch her breath between

dances, one of her cousin's cronies, Mrs. Torrington-Gower, sidled up to her, saying, "I don't believe her ladyship has ever looked lovelier than she does tonight."

"I am obliged to agree with you, ma'am," Arabella replied, but her attention was focused on her husband in laughing conversation with the Archduchess Catherine and Lady Hertford.

"It might benefit you too to follow in her footsteps and consult Dr. Manfred in Wimpole Street, if you hope to keep your husband happy."

At last Arabella gave the woman her full attention. "Dr. Manfred?"

Mrs. Torrington-Gower lowered her voice. "His Oil of Amaranthe does wonders for a woman."

"Indeed? Personally I vouch by Dr. Considine of Folkestone. Nothing is more effective for preserving one's youth than his Balm of Hesperides."

The woman considered Arabella for a long moment before she answered thoughtfully. "I daresay that accounts for *your* transformation, my lady."

"Precisely," Arabella replied with perfect seriousness, but she smiled impishly when the woman rushed away, no doubt to impart the remarkable *on dit* to Kitty.

"From the smile on your face, am I to assume you're enjoying your own diversion, Belle?"

Arabella whirled around on her heel when she heard her husband's voice. "It would be difficult not to: it is such a great success."

His eyes were alight with amusement, something that unaccountably irritated her. "I notice you're in great demand, and rightly so, but do I dare to hope you've reserved a dance for me?"

"It would be cork-brained of us not to dance together. We mustn't lose sight of the object of our marriage, must we?"

The amusement faded from his eyes, which then took on their usual somber hue. "Ah yes, it's just as well, we're so good at pretending."

He whirled her into the waltzing throng on the dance floor, observed by many admiring eyes. On so many previous occasions, it had been Arabella who had watched elegant ladies and their suave beaux dance in an ever-changing kaleidoscope of color, tapping her foot and wishing she could take part too. Now, with Lucian holding her close, she would trade this triumph just for his fond regard.

Everyone was breathless when the waltz ended, and as always, the enforced intimacy with her husband left Arabella with churning emotions. At that moment she felt she couldn't face another partner or make light conversation with her guests. Instead she went to seek a little air and a few minutes alone with her thoughts.

She was halfway down the stairs when she discovered that Lucian was following her. "Belle, are you feeling offish?" he asked, and he sounded truly concerned.

"No, I thank you, merely a bit overcome with the heat."

He joined her, nevertheless, in the downstairs hall with the strains of music drifting down to them. When she reached the hall, she turned to face her husband at last, hoping her feelings for him were not too obviously displayed on her face.

"Belle, I don't believe I've told you how beautiful you look this evening."

She hoped her cheeks didn't betray her true feelings, but her heart certainly fluttered at his unexpected praise, spoken so sincerely. "No one has ever called me beautiful before."

"There's no doubt that you are tonight."

Slowly, she raised her eyes to meet his. Was it admiration she saw in their cold gray depths or mockery? She couldn't be sure, but she was certain he was going to kiss her, and every nerve in her body quivered in anticipation. His hands grasped her around the waist, and she moaned. When his lips met hers, she was ready, and her response was immediate. He couldn't fail to be aware of it.

From his first touch desire ripped through her body, sending her blood coursing hotly through her veins. She sensed he was similarly aroused, and all at once he pulled her more firmly against him, the kiss deepening, threatening to bruise her lips and weaken any will she might have had to resist.

Somewhere nearby a guest chuckled as she passed by. The kiss might have lasted a minute or an eternity, but when he drew away, the look in his eyes was now one of shock, mirroring her own.

"So this is where our respective partners are lurking. How unfashionable you are to keep company with your own wife."

The soft, dulcet tone was unmistakable. Arabella turned her startled gaze on Kitty, who was strolling down the stairs arm in arm with Count Gronski. Fury and heartache replaced the all too brief feeling of desire when she realized the kiss that had seared her with its fire had been solely for Kitty's benefit, not out of any need Lucian felt for her.

"I am to return to St. Petersburg on the morrow."

Arabella turned to Count Gronski, who led her to the side of the dance floor after the cotillion. She had followed the steps automatically, for her thoughts returned time and again to that all too brief moment of intimacy with Lucian. Despite the prosaic purpose of his embrace, she could almost believe his ardor equaled her own, and

176

she still ached for him, for a renewal of his touch. Her heart lurched when she caught sight of him, leading his aunt onto the floor for the next set, and when he paused to glance in her direction, she quickly averted her eyes for fear he might read her thoughts.

Arabella forced a conciliatory smile to her lips, and concentrated on attending the man at her side. "I shall certainly miss your company, Count Gronski."

"Will you?" His handsome face took on a look of intensity. "As much as I will miss you?"

Her smile faded a little. "You mustn't doubt it for a moment."

"Then, don't torture yourself, my dear Lady Carisbrooke. You could come with me."

She laughed uncomfortably. "How is that possible?"

"You might wish to run away with me."

For a moment she stared at him in astonishment before she gave him a bewildered smile. "That's unthinkable. Perhaps you have forgotten that I am a married woman."

"An unhappily married woman."

Alarmed, she snapped. "You presume too much, Count."

As she flicked open her fan in order to hide her expression of dismay, he went on, "It is clear to see in your eyes, my lady. The suffering, the misery. I am far too attuned to your every nuance to miss the truth."

"Moonshine!"

"There is no shame in wanting a better life for yourself. You can't have mistaken my deep regard for you, my lady, and if you come with me, I vow I shall spend the rest of my life making you the happiest woman in all the Russias."

Arabella made to move away from him, but he caught her by the arm and drew her back toward him, whispering, "When we are together at last, I will never neglect you. You will want for nothing, and I intend to make love to you every night."

The irony of his promise was not lost on her, and she threw back her head and laughed, startling the count, who said, "If I have been mistaken in my assumption, I beg your pardon, my lady."

She only laughed more, and observing her merriment and intrigued by it, the marquess claimed his wife's hand for the country-dance, commenting as he led her away, "Count Gronski evidently diverts you greatly."

"He amuses me, certainly."

"And what precisely did he say to cause such hilarity in you?"

Arabella faced him squarely on the edge of the dance floor, all amusement gone now. "He asked me to elope with him so he could make love to me every night."

Lord Carisbrooke's face grew dark. "The insolent puppy! I've a mind to call him out."

She cast him a mocking look from behind her fan. "Wouldn't that confer on our marriage a status it does not warrant?"

His answer was to thrust her into the midst of the set, led by the czar who was partnering Kitty Polstead. It occurred to Arabella that her cousin appeared more carefree and gay than she had for a long time and idly wondered what had caused the change in her.

"The victory celebrations are all but over, Lucian," she told him a moment later, "and I believe it is true to say you have succeeded in your goal. You have certainly wounded my cousin. There is nothing more to gain from the situation, so what do you intend to do now?"

"This is neither the time nor the place to discuss our marriage," was his tight-lipped reply, and as the orchestra struck up, Arabella knew she had to be content with that.

Chapter Twenty-one

*L*ong after her abigail had left the room, Arabella could not rest. The evening's events remained far too vividly in her mind to allow her to sleep, and she paced uneasily around the room, recalling Kitty's every expression and innuendo, Count Gronski's unexpected declaration of devotion, and more than anything else Lucian's display of passion. The kiss might have been only an act to annoy Kitty, but it had certainly unleashed in Arabella all the emotions she had for so long locked up inside her.

If she did not harbor such longings for a man who was impervious to her, she might have derived great satisfaction from the fact she had become a social success. She assumed her husband would savor gratification from the evening's events. His plan had succeeded beyond all expectations, and it was certain her own personal triumph had put Kitty's nose out of joint, just as it was supposed to do.

If only, Arabella thought, she could gain something from the situation. Not even social success or the declaration of devotion from a handsome Russian could fulfill her yearning, when all she wanted was the love of a man she had adored from afar for so long, someone whose affection was only directed toward Kitty. Kitty, who was undeserving of anyone's devotion.

From the depths of her melancholy, Arabella understood

perfectly how he felt; her own love was just as hopeless. Not even the appearance of a congenial marriage could compensate for the reality, for she was only too well aware even that was about to end.

Eventually she did drift into an uneasy sleep, only to be awakened by her bedchamber door being thrust back so violently it banged against the wall. Arabella sat up with a start, her sleep-filled eyes clearing after a few seconds to see Lucian standing in the doorway, swaying slightly on his heels.

"What do you want?" she asked in a shocked whisper.

He staggered into the room. "What every man wants—to enjoy his wife's company," he muttered, "in your case so generously bestowed on others."

She shrank back against the headboard of the four-poster. "Lucian, have a care. . . ."

He laughed nastily. "No need to act the innocent with me of all people, my proud beauty. Count Gronski isn't the only gentleman capable of making love to you every night. I can make love to you all day too if that's what you wish."

He laughed again, and Arabella's heart began to thud loudly against her ribs. "Lucian," she repeated, this time in a warning tone.

He lunged toward her, missed her entirely, and tumbled headlong across the bed into a drunken stupor. For a moment Arabella remained shocked into immobility, but when she accepted that he wasn't going to move again, she slithered out of the bed, gazing down at the man she had married.

"My darling, dearest husband," she whispered before she bent down to kiss first his forehead and then his lips. "If only you knew how much I love you."

His answer was a resounding snore. With a heartfelt sigh, she pulled up the sheet to cover him and withdrew to a nearby daybed from which she could observe him. She was able to enjoy watching every facet of his features, the aristocratic nose, the proud chin now shadowed with an incipient beard. His dark lashes fanned out on his high cheekbones, obliterating the habitual coldness in his eyes that could, at will, display a smoldering passion. In repose, she detected no anger or wish for revenge, only a handsome countenance that hid the remarkable wit of the man she had come to love so much.

Arabella awoke with a start, taking a second or two to recall why she was sleeping on the daybed, and then she realized the four-poster was empty. She sat up with a shock to discover Lucian standing over her, his eyes strangely dark, the expression on his unshaven face one of consternation and dismay.

"Tell me what happened last night," he demanded.

"Nothing. Nothing at all," she replied, and the tension that suffused his entire body ebbed away before her eyes. His relief was palpable. "You were foxed and simply fell into a stupor across my bed."

He sank down on the edge of the daybed, covering his face with his hands. "I am so ashamed, Belle. I have little recollection of what happened, but I bitterly regret my behavior."

Arabella had never witnessed him displaying so great a humility before, and that in itself was disturbing. She slipped off the daybed and went to stand against the wall by the window, pulling her shawl closer around her. "You have no need to apologize so profusely. You were foxed, and in any event, you have every right to come into your wife's bedchamber whenever you please."

He raised his head slowly, and she was forced to turn away from so intent a look. Instead she gazed out of the window, across the garden, which had bloomed into a mad riot of color since her arrival. The truth of the matter was that she had grown to like very much indeed being Lady Carisbrooke, and wanted desperately to continue. He might no longer want her. He certainly did not care for her, but she didn't relish the humiliation of being abandoned so soon after their marriage. Even if it meant the heartache of continuous pretense, it was a price she was more than willing to pay to remain at his side, to love him as always from afar.

The sound of rustling indicated he had moved, and a moment later she felt his breath close to her cheek. He put his hands on her shoulders, and it was all she could do to stop herself melting back against him, to allow his ever-present vitality to communicate itself to her. Even before he touched her, she was infused with an ardor it was growing ever more difficult to conceal.

"I'm quite sober now, Belle," he whispered, his lips against her ear, his hands heating her flesh as they began to rove gently over her body.

His touch sent a frisson of rapture through her, and unable to hold herself aloof from him any longer, she turned around, gazing deep into his eyes. This was not for Kitty's sake; it couldn't possibly be. A moment later she was in his arms, being pressed against his chest, his lips fastening on hers, claiming them with a passion that almost took her breath away.

Her response once unleashed was as instantaneous as before, the warm rush of passion flowing through her veins a rising tide about to engulf her. When his lips began to move along her cheek to press against the long line of her throat, Arabella started a journey of discovery of her own.

The invitation cards were spread across the surface of Arabella's *bonheur du jour*. She moved them to and fro separating them into three piles, those to refuse, those to accept, and the ones about which she would have to consult Lucian.

Whenever she thought about him, a smile came to her lips. The memory of what had occurred between them kept interrupting her thoughts and her actions. There could be no annulment now, only a very expensive divorce arranged by a special act of Parliament. Somehow she suspected such a fiercely proud man would not want to take that option.

"My lady, Lady Polstead is here and asks to see you."

Arabella started out of her thoughts. She hadn't heard the footman enter the small sitting room, even though he must have first knocked on the door. "Lady Polstead?" she repeated, feeling stupid.

Of all people, Kitty was the last one she wanted to see today. She didn't wish to be reminded of her husband's obsession with her cousin, not now, certainly not so soon after those heavenly hours spent in his arms, when she was able to pretend he cared for her a little. She didn't need Kitty's presence to remind her it really wasn't so and never would be.

"My lady?" the footman inquired, gazing at her curiously.

Arabella sighed and answered in a dull tone, "Show her in, Timton."

When Kitty was ushered in a few moments later, Arabella was outwardly composed and her cousin couldn't possibly have guessed her inner turmoil.

"Kitty," she greeted her with a smile. "How good to see you."

"I was passing close by and thought I must call in to tell you what a wonderful diversion you hosted last night. I truly am proud of all you've achieved, Bella. I'm sure you're aware the ball is the talk of the town."

"Thank you, Kitty. It's kind of you to take the time to

come and tell me. As you can imagine, I've scarcely had time to note the outcome."

Lady Polstead sat down on a sofa, appearing supremely at ease. Arabella could only marvel at her, suspicious of what appeared to be change of heart. "I couldn't help but notice the partiality that very handsome Count Gronski showed toward you." Arabella looked away as her cousin methodically stripped off her York kid gloves. "Now you have a gallant of your own, I do hope you will find it in your heart to understand my situation."

"The friendship Count Gronski has accorded me bears no resemblance to the one you enjoyed with my husband," Arabella replied with extreme embarrassment.

Suddenly her cousin looked coy. "You are bound to own, though, there is a certain irony in finding ourselves in similar situations."

"I have done nothing to encourage the count to believe I care for him."

"Oh, Bella, there is no need to come the artful with me, my dear. Count Gronski has been most forthcoming in his admiration, and it has not escaped my attention that your response to his interest has been no less ardent."

"You are mistaken, Kitty."

"When I was on my way here, I had it in mind you would be experiencing a feeling of despair today, as I know he is returning to St. Petersburg."

"Yes, he is, and I shall miss his company, as will so many of us who have been privileged to enjoy his society."

Lady Polstead toyed with her gloves. "So . . . you do not intend to go with him?"

Arabella began to feel agitated. "Indeed not."

"Then, I declare you a fool, Bella, to turn your back on a man who adores you so completely."

"Have you forgotten I am married to Carisbrooke?"

Her cousin laughed harshly. "That would be impossible, and you have done very well. Very well indeed. I had no notion you could be so resourceful."

Arabella sat down at last, on the edge of a chair. "Am I to feel flattered, Kitty? Recall, I had so many opportunities to run your household before I married Carisbrooke."

"Ah yes. I really must give myself more credit for your recent successes." For a moment or two she considered her gloves again before going on. "You and I have always been able to be honest with each other, and I deem we should continue that admirable trait, don't you agree?"

"I have always believed in honesty, Kitty."

"I confess, you and Carisbrooke look good together, but although your acquaintances believe you are a perfect match, in truth, you are not in the least suited to such a passionate man."

"How do you know that, Kitty?" Arabella found the courage to ask.

"Because I am quite persuaded you are aware your husband is still very much devoted to me."

Arabella opened her fan, and in the midst of her unease heard herself saying, "That was undoubtedly so before he met me, and I shall always be indebted to you for the opportunity you afforded me to become acquainted with my husband, but it must be obvious to you, he has undergone a change of heart. There can be no doubt he loves me."

Lady Polstead laughed again, but now there was a harsh undertone to it. "Bella, Bella, I can't possibly boast of it to anyone, but there is no need for you to pretend with me...."

"My wife isn't pretending," the marquess told her.

Arabella looked past her cousin in alarm to see her husband in the doorway of the drawing room, holding open the door. Then she smiled with relief at the interruption. He cast her a quick, reassuring glance that warmed her heart before coming further into the room and addressing Lady Polstead again.

"It's true to say the circumstances of our wedding were unusual, but since our marriage, I have come to love your cousin very much." Lady Polstead's face took on a look of abhorrence. "It isn't just her youth and beauty that enthrall me, but her wit and generosity of spirit. In other words, my dear, she is the complete opposite of you. Perhaps I looked past the glitter that briefly dazzled me and found the real gold beyond."

A lump began to form in Arabella's throat and tears glistened on her lashes as her cousin gathered up her reticule and jumped to her feet, suddenly all haste. She smiled thinly at Arabella and then at the marquess. "There is nothing left for me to say except to wish you happy. Good day to you both."

She hurried to the door, her head held high, but her smile had gone. When she entered the hall, her waiting maidservant jumped to her feet and followed wordlessly, instinctively aware of her mistress's ill humor. Lady Polstead's head footman was waiting by the door of the carriage. When she looked up at him, her face was a mask of fury.

"She'll have to go," she spat as she climbed into the carriage.

Arabella waited until Kitty was well away before she turned to Lucian and, feeling rather awkward, said, "Thank you for saying that."

The marquess was frowning at the door, but now he looked at his wife. "We really need to talk about this."

Panic now combined with all the other emotions she had been experiencing that morning. "Not now, Lucian," she begged. "I'm engaged to join Lady Brimston for luncheon."

Before he could detain her further, she hurried out of the room, putting off the evil moment for a little while longer.

When Arabella had exhausted every reason to stay away from Carisbrooke House, she dismissed the carriage and, accompanied by her maidservant, began to walk disconsolately back to Grosvenor Square, aware she could not postpone the inevitable confrontation a moment longer.

As she turned the corner into the square, so deep were her thoughts, she scarcely noticed the carriage with curtained windows standing there. Without warning, just as she was passing, the carriage door flew open, a man sprang out and grabbed hold of Arabella. She cried out, but it all happened so quickly and unexpectedly not even her abigail could do anything but stand and watch in a shocked silence. The moment Arabella had been bundled into the carriage, it sped off, leaving the maidservant speechless on the pavement.

At the same time as the carriage sped away, a brand-new racing curricle passed it going in the opposite direction. It came to a halt outside Carisbrooke House, as the marquess came down the steps to greet his cousin.

"Came to show you m'new carriage," Henry Brimston called out as he climbed down from the box.

"It's quite splendid, Monk. You're acquiring fine taste at last. I only wish I had time to take a turn in it, but I'm waiting for Arabella to come home."

The young man looked perplexed and scratched his head. "Oddest thing, Carisbrooke. I could vouch I saw her ladyship being forced into a carriage at the corner just now."

The marquess's welcoming smile faded into a frown. "What the devil! Are you sure?"

"Couldn't mistake Lady C."

His cousin was still frowning fiercely when the abigail came running down the street screaming. "Help! Help! My lord, her ladyship has been abducted right in front of my very eyes!"

She pointed in the direction the carriage had taken with an unsteady finger. The marquess's face took on a horrified look before he snatched the riding whip from his cousin's hand and jumped onto the box of the curricle.

"Shall I come . . . ?" Monk asked, but his cousin had already whipped up the horses and was speeding off in the same direction as the carriage.

Chapter Twenty-two

"*W*hat is going on?" Arabella demanded in an unsteady voice as the carriage incarcerating her raced off the moment the door slammed shut.

The man facing her didn't reply. He was wearing an all-enveloping frieze coat and a muffler obscured the lower part of his face.

"Where are you taking me? I demand to know," she persisted, becoming even more agitated in the face of his silence.

"My, my," the man answered at last in a mocking tone. "We 'ave become toplofty 'aven't we?"

In the midst of her terror, Arabella was sure she recognized some element in his voice, but full enlightenment eluded her, perhaps because she was so scared her mind refused to function properly.

Having recovered from the immediate shock of being forced into the carriage, almost as soon as it set off, Arabella fought hard to contain her panic, to think rationally, to discover a way out of this terrifying situation.

For a brief moment she'd wondered if Count Gronski had arranged for her to be abducted, and then she dismissed the notion as too ludicrous. Vladimir Gronski was no hothead. He was a diplomat, and in any event he wouldn't have wished to alarm her in this manner. If the count had been the perpetrator of the outrage, he'd have been present in the carriage waiting for her. She even toyed with the idea that someone from the Jolly Hangman might be behind the wheeze, but doubted if any of that rabble were clever enough to arrange an abduction. There was only one explanation, and having so decided, she leaned toward the fellow, who was taking brief, nervous glances from behind the curtains.

"I believe you have mistaken my identity for that of someone else. I am Lady Carisbrooke. My husband is the Marquess of Carisbrooke. He's a gentleman of great consequence, and I know he would be willing to reward you handsomely for my return."

Her abductor laughed behind the muffler. "I know exactly who you are, *my lady.*"

Suddenly an awful thought came into her mind. Lucian could be the one behind this outrage. *Lucian.* Arabella sank back into the squabs, trying to deny the treacherous suspicion that refused to be dismissed.

Because he couldn't have the annulment he'd originally planned, this might be his answer to the problem his marriage now presented. *And she had given him the notion.* It was she who had told him Count Gronski asked her to go away with him. When he confided in one or two tattle baskets the reason for her disappearance, the story would spread like fire on tinder, through the ranks of the ton.

Uttering a groan of dismay, she pulled back the curtain obscuring the window. The familiar streets had given way to insalubrious neighborhoods from which malodorous smells drifted into the carriage. It was going too fast to allow her to jump out, an option she quickly discounted. Just as her captor snatched the curtain from her grasp and closed it again, she caught a glimpse of the river, running parallel to the road.

As she shrank back once more she closed her eyes to

force back tears of despair squeezing through her lids and reflected that she didn't care what happened to her now if Lucian wanted his freedom so desperately he'd employ someone to do away with her. Perhaps now Kitty was suitably chastened he had hopes of rekindling their relationship. Kitty might even have intimated she was willing to leave Sir Andrew after all and go away with him. The scandal over her own disappearance would, in all probability, deflect the furor from them.

When the carriage came to a halt at last, Arabella was so distraught over Lucian's perceived betrayal, she had no spirit left with which to fight. Her captor thrust open the door and pulled her onto what she discovered was a quay, alongside a full-masted East Indiaman.

The fate planned for her was immediately obvious. She'd be sold into slavery on some far distant shore by the master of the ship. That prospect was hard enough to accept, although her husband's assumed treachery was the truly unbearable part. Her gentle and passionate lover had planned this dreadful fate, perhaps even as he made love to her the night before.

"Oh, Lucian," she sighed, his name uttered as a sibilant whisper. "I do love you so."

Her captor tugged at her sleeve, and she stumbled forward at the same moment Lord Brimston's new racing curricle clattered to a halt behind the carriage.

The noise occasioned the man to swing around, loosening his hold on his prisoner. Arabella, whose despair turned to hope, saw her husband jump down and run onto the quay.

"Unhand her, you muckworm!" he roared, wielding the riding whip to such good effect the villain overbalanced and with a cry fell backward into the Thames.

Arabella's face was transformed from despair to joy,

and she beamed at last. "Lucian! Oh, Lucian, I'm so glad to see you."

He turned away from her adversary, who was struggling in his frieze coat to stay afloat. "What did he do to you?" he asked tersely as he examined her face.

"Nothing. Nothing at all."

He relaxed visibly and then glanced up, becoming wary as several seamen started to walk down the gangway. He took her hand in his and led her at a run to the curricle. "Let's get away from here."

"Oh yes, please!"

He lifted her onto the box, jumped up next to her, and with one flick of his whip set the team in motion before the seamen even reached the quay. Arabella couldn't take her eyes off her husband. Her face glowed.

"You came! You rescued me!"

"You can thank Monk for my speed. He arrived with this splendid contraption and team just as your abigail reached us in a state of the hysterics."

She glanced back as the docks melted into the distance, before turning to beseech her husband, "I must beg your pardon for doubting you, Lucian. I thought all this was your notion."

He paused to cast her a frowning glance before turning his attention to negotiating the traffic. There was a great deal of it on the road, private carriages of all kinds, wagons and hackney carriages. His skill in avoiding them all while at the same time keeping up his speed always invited her admiration. Today his prowess as a whipster had been crucial in their escape.

"Me!" he cried. "Why would I want to have you abducted?"

She knew her cheeks were growing pink as she looked away from him. "Because you can no longer obtain an annulment of our marriage."

He stopped the curricle so abruptly, she jerked forward in her seat. "I don't want an annulment."

Arabella straightened her bonnet and then looked up into his face, searching it for signs of insincerity. "Don't you, Lucian?"

He pulled her into his arms, and she laid her head against his chest. "I spoke the truth this morning, Belle. I have come to love you very much. What I felt for your cousin was a mere bagatelle compared to my overwhelming devotion to you. Can you possibly put the unfortunate start to our relationship out of your mind and begin anew?"

"There's no need. I've loved you all along."

He held her away from him, his searching look taking in every facet of her features. "I don't deserve you."

His lips touched hers lightly, and at that moment they both forgot entirely that they could clearly be seen by all who passed. Clutched in each other's arms, they kissed until they were breathless. Then, laughing with new-found joy, they held each other tight as if they would never let go. Neither was aware of a barouche passing by, or of one of the ladies traveling in it who was craning her neck to get a better view of the embracing pair.

"Isn't that your nephew Carisbrooke?" the woman asked of her companion.

Lady Brimston smiled with satisfaction. "Yes, I believe it is."

"He's kissing his wife in full public view!"

"How very old-fashioned of him," her ladyship replied, still smiling as the barouche passed out of sight, "but at least we can be sure it's for their very own sakes and no one else's!"

"Do you really have to leave now?" Arabella asked her husband, drawing him closer to her again and burying her hands in the density of his dark curls.

193

He kissed her briefly on the tip of her nose, answering, "You're making it prodigiously difficult for me, but I do need to return the curricle and team to my cousin and tender some kind of explanation for what happened this morning."

"Later," she insisted.

Much later, he climbed out of the four-poster telling her, "While I'm gone have your abigail pack a few boxes." In response to her quizzical look he asked, "How would you like to go down to Auden End for a delayed honeymoon?"

Arabella gasped as she sat up, clutching the sheet against her. "We can't, Lucian, not now. We have so many engagements already arranged."

"Can't we say you're indisposed and need a long period of rustication to recover your health and spirits?"

She chuckled and looked bashful. "We can't! If I cry off on those grounds, everyone will think I'm increasing!"

He leaned over and kissed her briefly again. "Let them think what they will. I'll be back in time to travel down. I can't wait to show you Auden End." He backed away from the bed, pulling on his clothes in a haphazard manner quite unlike his usual fastidiousness. "I don't mean to share you with another soul for the next month or more."

She sank back into the huge feather pillows. "That sounds like absolute bliss."

"It will be."

She watched with great pleasure as he folded his neck cloth into place and blushed when he smiled at her through the looking glass.

"Lucian, when you were bosky, you boasted if Count Gronski could make love to me all night you would do so all day too. . . ."

He turned on his heel to face her as he buttoned his
194

waistcoat. "If you believe it was an idle boast," he told her with mock seriousness, "just wait until I get you to Auden End."

"I don't know if I have patience enough to wait that long!"

"If I'd known you were such a passionate baggage, I wouldn't have troubled to restrain myself for such a long time."

"Was that a difficult task?"

"More arduous than I was willing to own."

All at once she frowned as she gazed up at the brocade tester above her head, "Lucian, who do you think had me abducted if it wasn't Count Gronski?"

He paused as he shrugged into his coat then continued to fasten it before he leaned over to kiss her. "Why cudgel your brain? You are quite safe now."

"Someone went to a good deal of trouble."

As he gazed down at her, his eyes became clouded. "I recognized the villain when he fell into the river: he is your cousin's head footman."

Arabella was busily supervising the packing of her boxes, wondering how little she need take to Auden End when a flustered house steward came into the room.

"I do beg your pardon, my lady, for disturbing you. . . ."

"Don't trouble to pack the chiffons. I'll need more sturdy garb for the country," she told her abigail before turning to the house steward to ask, "What's amiss, Hudson? You look to be in something of a fidge."

"Lady Polstead is here, my lady, to see his lordship, but I can't find him anywhere in the house, and she is most insistent that she speak with him."

Arabella's ready smile faded. Ever since Lucian had left to return Monk's curricle, she had brooded on his revelation. It was doubly wounding because, for all her

195

faults, she would never have believed Kitty capable of such wickedness. However, after dwelling on the matter for some time, she decided she would permit no one to interfere with her newfound happiness. Only her separation from Molly, which looked set to continue, cast a shadow over the future.

"Lady Polstead," she repeated, more to herself than to the lackey.

"Yes, my lady. What should I tell her?"

She clasped her hands together in front of her and took a deep breath. "I'll come down and see her myself."

Temple, Kitty's abigail, was sitting primly in the hall, and when Arabella walked through, the woman started visibly. In the small sitting room Kitty Polstead was standing by the window, gazing out into the garden. When she heard footsteps, she turned and there was a smile on her lips that faded abruptly the moment she saw her cousin.

"Bella!" she cried.

"I understand you wanted to see my husband, but I'm afraid he is not at home."

All color drained from her face, and she swayed where she stood. Arabella rushed to her then, her coolness giving way to alarm as she cried, "Kitty!" She assisted her cousin to the sofa before calling the waiting abigail. "Your mistress has swooned and needs your help."

The maidservant held a vinaigrette to her mistress's nose. Kitty's eyes fluttered open as Arabella hovered close by, and then the woman sat up, pushing her maidservant away. "This is all your fault, Temple! I knew you'd laced me too tight!"

The maidservant shrank away just as the marquess appeared in the doorway to his wife's profound relief. She rushed over to him, saying quickly, "My cousin

196

called in to see you, Lucian, but has taken badly in the meantime."

He kept a protective arm around her waist while never taking his eyes from Kitty. "A condition brought on by shock. No doubt, she didn't expect to see *you* here."

"Oh, I feel as sick as a cushion," Lady Polstead complained.

The marquess walked farther into the room, peering at the woman he had once professed to have loved. "You do look hag-ridden, my dear, positively bracket-faced."

Kitty Polstead cringed away from him. "How cruel you are to someone who is so badly out of curl."

"But it's true! Most alarming. You really must have a care, my lady, else you begin to look *old*."

"Oh!"

Arabella was forced to suppress a chuckle behind her hand as her husband added. "If I were a quack, I'd recommend a prolonged rustication to recoup your looks and spirits."

The woman swung her legs over the side of the sofa. "I'm considering a visit to Folkestone—the sea air—Dr. Considine."

She walked past them unsteadily, and as she did so, the marquess went on mercilessly. "I'm going to send a carriage to Thirlmere to collect your daughter. Arabella and I want her to stay with us in the country for a lengthy visit. I don't expect to receive any objections from you."

Kitty didn't reply, but when she reached the door, Lucian added, "Lady Polstead, if any harm should come to my wife, even of the most superficial nature, I shall know where to lay the blame."

She paused to glance at them, her face ashen, her eyes dull, and at that moment Arabella pitied her cousin with all her heart. As soon as she had gone, Arabella threw her arms around her husband's neck.

"Thank you, my love. Thank you for Molly. Thank you for everything."

He looked down at her, and she wondered why she had ever thought his eyes cold. Just then they were filled with warmth, and it was directed only toward her.

"I intend to do everything in my power to make you happy from now on."

"You have already made me very happy indeed."

"Then, I am more fortunate than I deserve. Come along, my lovely," he added as he ushered her toward the door. "The quicker we leave, the sooner we are able to begin the rest of our lives together. I don't want to waste a moment more!"

Want to know a secret?
It's sexy, informative, fun, and FREE!!!

❧ PILLOW TALK ❧

Join Pillow Talk and get advance information and sneak peeks at the best in romance coming from Ballantine. All you have to do is fill out the information below!

♥ My top five favorite authors are: _____

_____

_____

_____

_____

♥ Number of books I buy per month: ❏ 0-2 ❏ 3-5 ❏ 6 or more

♥ Preference: ❏ Regency Romance ❏ Historical Romance
　　　　　　❏ Contemporary Romance ❏ Other

♥ I read books by new authors: ❏ frequently ❏ sometimes ❏ rarely

Please print clearly:
Name _____

Address_____

City/State/Zip_____

Don't forget to visit us at
www.randomhouse.com/BB/loveletters

regency

NOW IN PAPERBACK

The *New York Times* hardcover bestseller

SOMEONE LIKE YOU
by Elaine Coffman

"An emotionally satiating work that is
an instant keeper . . ."
—*Affaire de Coeur*

"An intensely moving tale of emotional growth
and discovery. Once again, Mrs. Coffman spins
a complex tapestry of the human heart,
a vivid portrayal of life and
the grace and redemption of love."
—*Romantic Times*

In this stirring romance set in nineteeth-century
Texas, a mystery man who appears to be a down-on-
his-luck cowboy and a beautiful young "spinster" hid-
ing a secret past of her own dare to reach for love.
Hailed for the richness and complexity of her work,
Elaine Coffman demonstrates yet again why she is one
of the most beloved romance writers.

On sale now